Aya Dane

Mhani Alaoui

Interlink Books

An imprint of Interlink Publishing Group, Inc.
Northampton, Massachusetts

First published 2019 by

Interlink Books
An imprint of Interlink Publishing Group, Inc.
46 Crosby Street, Northampton, MA 01060
www.interlinkbooks.com

Library of Congress Cataloging-in-Publication Data:
Names: Alaoui, Mhani, author.
Title: Aya Dane / by Mhani Alaoui.
Description: Northampton MA : Interlink Books, an imprint of
    Interlink Publishing Group Inc., [2019]
Identifiers: LCCN 2018036320 | ISBN 9781623719685
Classification: LCC PR9170.M53 A525 2019 | DDC 823/.92--dc23
LC record available at https://lccn.loc.gov/2018036320

Printed and bound in the United States of America

To request our complete 48-page, full-color catalog, please call us toll
free at 1-800-238-LINK, visit our website at www.interlinkbooks.com or
write Interlink Publishing, 46 Crosby Street, Northampton, MA 01060
e-mail: info@interlinkbooks.com

to Amine

Aya Dane

one

My name is Aya Dane.

If you're reading these words, it means I've left my life behind. It means that, once you've heard news of my disappearance, you've entered my studio of your own free will and taken what you need.

First, you look through my old pictures, my clothes, my books. Then, with barely concealed excitement, you walk into my studio and set your eyes upon what means the most to me—my work. You sift through the colors, the browns, purples and yellows, the rare burgundy and proud ochre. You touch the transformed material, wood, iron, glass, cloth, plastic that are my labor.

You look at my work, sprawled and abandoned before you, and wonder wherein lay the secret of my talent. You won't feel any shame, for it's your right, is it not, to take apart a life once its owner has disappeared.

Your curiosity leads you deeper into my work, into the mechanics of my art and the complexities of its composition. Then, because that's what interests you the most in the end and because the silence and crimson light of my studio can be stifling, you begin looking for closed boxes and hidden caches.

You begin to believe that there must be more than meets the eye, and, of course, you are right. You open drawers, rummage through the discarded objects at the back of the studio, move aside carpets and furniture, push aside the small, absurd details that we call a life. Until, finally, you find what you were looking for.

Does a sense of entitlement soothe any guilt pangs you might have at stripping my home bare, at discarding my intimacy? Does your position of power enable your curiosity, justify your violations?

But then, who am I to throw the first stone? After all, was I not responsible for having left so abruptly? Hasn't my disappearance left my life without protection, up for grabs?

And now, you really don't care anymore, because you have found what you came for. Perhaps you didn't even know this was what you came for until you found it.

You gaze at a lined notebook you discover at the bottom of a box underneath my bed. *Aya Dane had many secrets*, the words on the pages whisper to you. You take out the notebook, gently, as though it could break. You hold it, tightly, like the predator holding its victim close lest she run away. You breathe, your heartbeat impossible to control.

Only then do you sit down in the leather chair with a cup of tea steaming on the table in front of you, and truly look at the pages lying between your hands.

No one interrupts you, for you claimed you were an old friend, an insurance agent, a private detective, a concerned doctor. And you begin to read.

This is my story, lying open in your hands.

I never planned on writing it down. I wrote these pages in my notebook because of you. Because of the memories that came back to me after fifteen years of forgetfulness. And they came back with force, fierceness, vengeance. They came back in the guise of a voice that whispered to me in the dead of night, when the day's dust had settled.

I don't know why or how I began to remember. I only know for certain that my memories returned, that a voice spoke for me, and *I* transformed into *she*, after I heard the pianist play.

two

The pianist's song rang all around her. Notes hung in the air as she walked quickly through the plush lobby of David's apartment building. They followed her, tugged at her, burst against the back of her head, as she hurried out of the building.

She had spent the night at David's. It wasn't often that Aya was willing to leave her place and sleep in another bed. There were certain evening rituals she had to do in order to fall asleep. So it was difficult for her to spend a night anywhere else than at her own place. But he had asked her to come over. He had said it was important, that it was time she ventured out of her hole and come to him. There was something a bit cold about his tone, and words. But, behind his detachment, Aya sensed genuine worry, a gentleness, which drew her to him.

Aya was awake and David asleep when his next-door neighbor, a ghostlike, elusive man, placed his hands on the keyboard of the piano in the lobby and began to play a song, over and over. The song troubled her. It was a Leonard Cohen ballad she hadn't heard since she was a child, in her home in Tangiers. She sat up and listened quietly, barely breathing or moving. Finally, the tune's repetitiveness, its soft, lonesome cruelty, overwhelmed her. She grabbed her clothes and ran out of David's apartment.

Struggling to control the memories that had risen out of the pianist's dark tune, she pulled on her gloves, pushed the heavy revolving doors at the end of the building's entry hall, and stepped out onto the sidewalk.

A damp chill seeped into the marrow of her bones. She zipped up her coat against the cold and looked around at the quiet, empty streets. It was a holiday. Today would be a day of feasting and warm fires. But it was still very early in the morning, so she could avoid human contact in the streets. She looked up at the high windows and curved balconies lining the brownstones of the Back Bay, and imagined the homes as they would be later that day. Long tables laden with food, silver candelabra and crystal vases filled with flowers. Elegant, unattainable figures moving lightly between tables and balconies.

She walked under the snow-covered trees, alongside whitened bushes to her right, then turned north and continued until she reached the Charles River. Crossing Harvard Bridge into Cambridge, she lowered her head against the iciness rising from the river below, trapped in its white silence. Leaving the bridge, she let the empty streets guide her through their maze. The high-rises and gilded brownstones of Boston rose behind her, as her steps crunched the thin layer of snow covering the soft green grass that lined the bay of the Charles River.

Her phone rang.

It was David. "Daoud" as she liked to whisper to him when they were in bed together, or just sitting, facing one another, in almost complete silence, in the penumbra of her home. Daoud, for the alluring appeal and incomprehensible syllables that caused him, for reasons he could not comprehend but that she could, to shiver in disgust.

"You left without saying goodbye."

Her breath shortened and she tightened her grip on the phone. His tone was concerned, poised.

"The pianist woke me up. And I didn't want to wake you."

"What pianist?"

"The blind pianist who lives in your building."

"What blind pianist, Aya?"

"The one who plays Duke Ellington and Leonard Cohen. Whose apartment is next to yours."

"There is no blind pianist on my floor."

Aya held back her reply. David was oblivious to details, while she noticed every single, excruciating thing. She shifted topics.

"I have a canvas waiting for me, dying in the light of day."

"A canvas? Can't it wait?"

"No. It can't. Not this time."

"…This new project you're working on, it's not like the others."

"No, it's not."

"Why is it so special?"

"It isn't what it appears to be. It will change things."

"It sure is changing you. Ever since you began working on it, you haven't been yourself. I'm worried about you. You're taking your pills?"

"I'm home, David. I need to go."

She hung up.

Aya had reached the quaint Victorian house where she lived. The owners, a middle-aged couple in the tech business, had moved to San Francisco and rented her the house. But Aya decided to occupy the top floor only, because the rest of the

house, where the family once lived, felt too large, too unfamiliar and uncontrollable. She never lingered on the first
floor, but would quickly cross the foyer and climb the three
flights of stairs that led to the attic.

When she moved in, she had tried to live downstairs.
First, she had spent the night in the master bedroom. But
the wind howled against the maple trees, filling the window
with ominous shadows and rattling it incessantly. Then, she'd
tried the children's bedroom. Though she felt safer and more
tranquil in the smaller, squarer room, she still couldn't sleep,
bothered by the lack of light and the thin windows that
looked out onto the graying lawn. After that, she had tried
the living room, but its dark, dusty corners seemed to hide
monstrous lives in their folds.

So Aya had climbed the three flights of stairs that led
to the top floor of the house and pushed open the door into
the attic. Its slanted walls and curved ceiling pulsated peace
and quiet, a welcome anonymity. There she lived and worked,
diligently avoiding the rest of the house. The attic, she
thought, held the soul of this unknowable place. Sometimes,
she thought that dark and secret experiments were once con-
ducted there, under an all-seeing gaze, and that perhaps she
was its last, and darkest, one.

She pushed the key into the lock, turned it and entered.
With the owners' agreement, she had had high windows
installed in the exterior walls, so that a maximum amount of
light could come pouring in, during the greatest number of
hours. She had split the attic into two, very different parts. A
large glass panel that slid open in the middle cut the space in
two uneven halves. The smaller part extended into a balcony
overlooking the garden and the street below and was divided
into a bedroom, a living room with a fireplace, and a small

kitchen. That was her living area. A bookcase brimming with books covered an entire wall. She found some joy in the wrought-iron balcony and the old fireplace that could still nurture a fire. In front of the fireplace was an oak coffee table, covered in old magazines and melted candles. Between the coffee table and the fireplace were two worn, brown leather sofas. She couldn't remember where she bought the sofas or the coffee table, but it must have been at the antique store not far from the house. The other, larger, part of the attic was her art studio, where light came streaming in, where she kept her canvases and art supplies. She liked to leave a small light burning there at night. It comforted her, let her hold onto the remains of the spent day, kept sounds and fears at bay. She put down her bag and coat and went into the kitchen to prepare some tea.

———

Water boiled, odorless and colorless, in the curved copper teapot. A pinch of Chinese gunpowder tea, rubbed between her fingers, mint leaves, strewn into the boiling water, their fragrance, fresh and cool, mingling with the black tea and the hot water. She pushed the sugar in, through the mint leaves, through the Chinese gunpowder tea and into the darkness beneath as some of its crystalline sweetness stuck to her fingertips. She watched as the tea simmered and closed her eyes to take in its peculiar, incomparable scent. Her own, private, secret Orient in the dark interior of a rounded teapot… On the rare occasions when she had guests over, she would offer regular tea, or chamomile or verbena, but she never offered them the Moroccan mint tea. The infrequent guests would joke that there was nothing of the East left in her, that she was completely Westernized. She would smile and pick up her glass of shiny white wine, while gold and blue arabesque figures danced and fissured behind her eyelids.

She drank the tea and felt its sweetness, its freshness, but also the darkness that lurked inside the copper teapot and now coursed through her body.

She did not drink this tea to remember the faraway fragrances of home. She did not drink it to awaken soft memories of the past. She drank this tea, alone, to touch the darkness at its heart, one that endlessly echoed inside her. Darkness that transformed into pain that burned behind her eyes and seared through her body.

three

When she was a little girl, Aya was afraid of the dark. When her mother tucked her in at night, she could never simply close her eyes and go to sleep, like other children could. Every night, she would ask her mother, "If I swim down the deepest depths of the ocean, will you come with me, will you come with me into the darkest darkness?" And every night her mother would answer, "I will come with you to the darkest, deepest darkness." And her mother would drink her mint tea and stroke her hair till she fell asleep. In the morning, when the sunlight hit the tiny room and the purple bougainvillea brushed against the window, Aya would find her mother's empty glass with the darkened grains of tea at the bottom, still wet.

four

It was the twenty-seventh of November, a day in the midst of a crisp autumn, broken by a snowfall. It was a day that Aya had shut tightly at the back of her mind every year for the past fifteen years. Her phone lit up and she saw she had received a text message. She pressed the icon, and the message, from an international number, popped up on the screen. For the past fifteen years, she had received a text from the same number; the same exact message, from the same exact international number. For the past fourteen years she would look at it, and then delete it.

> *As the fire burns,*
> *The journey becomes loss*
> *The departure, exile.*

She knew who had sent her the message. She knew it could only be from *him*. This year, once again, she glanced at the text and was about to delete it, when she noticed a difference. The fourteen previous messages had three lines. This one had four.

> *As the fire burns,*
> *The journey becomes loss*
> *The departure, exile.*
> *And the muñeca breaks.*

And the muñeca breaks. The muñeca. She shivered at the forgotten sound, at this word, that she hadn't heard in such a long time. A word that brought back the tenderness of childhood, of the special language that cradled a Tangiers childhood. Muñeca: the word for doll in both Spanish and Tangerine Arabic. It was a word that held in its lithe, graceful consonants all the language of love, affection and play between an older Tangiers generation, bred in the melodious Spanish ways and the aristocratic Andalusi lifestyle, and a younger one. Them. They, the forsaken ones. A word that temporarily mended the breaks between parents and grandparents who had been raised in the Moorish culture, and their children, a word astride the old and the new, the aristocratic and the impoverished, the sophisticated and the brutalized. A word that, to Aya, represented the endless dance of the two, the eternal back and forth where old and new spin and turn until they fade into unfettered loss.

Gradually, her thoughts wrapped around the word, hung on its letters, reached toward its curious presence. Why was the word there? This had to be deliberate, it couldn't be a mistake. What did it mean? What did *he*—it had to be him, who else could it be?—want from her still after all these years, when all she wanted was to be left alone.

Muñeca. She could remember one muñeca, and only vaguely; her doll, made of porcelain, as some precious dolls were at the time. It was a pretty little thing with curly blonde hair and a delicate red and black lace dress. But that was all she could remember. She tried to recall some other detail, a place or a scene, but could only conjure emptiness. And yet she sensed that the doll held a special meaning, even though she couldn't decipher it. She sensed that she had been attached to her muñeca, perhaps had even loved it.

For the past fourteen years, she had read the message and deleted it without answering. This year she couldn't bring herself to erase the message, but neither could she answer it. She saved the message and pushed the phone away. She had already wasted enough time on it. She had the most important work of her life to do. She rose and walked toward the glass paneling that separated her living space from her art studio and slid the doors open.

————————

She stood in front of the canvas. Canvases were one part of her work. They were its first emanation, which then crawled and spread out on the floor, in the form of installations made of glass, steel, brick, wood, debris. She didn't know in advance the shape or material each particular sculpture might take. But they derived from the canvas itself.

Her installations started by accident. She had been working on a painting of a boat drifting at sea, when a drop of blue paint fell on a glass container at her feet. The blue on the glass shimmered and seemed to reflect the light that came from the canvas, appeared to complete the trail of white and blue left by the lost boat in its wake. That was when her work transformed from painting to installation.

A woman's undulating brown hair would spill over onto a corroded metal container that Aya would then chisel to emulate the flow of hair. Eyelashes on closed eyes would become sheets of shredded paper, hanging from a wooden stick. The muscles on a bent back would become yellow foam threaded throughout by gauze and horizontal needles. The traditional Tangiers dress of heavy silk and gold thread became brown sand and colored glass. A work might be arranged like a crime scene or a funeral wake, or a haunting. And at the center of every piece, on the canvas's lower right-hand corner—on the right because it was reminiscent of Arabic writing and the lost traces of the Arabic alphabet—Aya placed a blood-red flower, aslant, asleep, made of painted porcelain.

This time, it would be different. This piece would be a painting, like her original work. Solely a canvas, which breathed back into itself all its broken fragments, its wood and metal shards.

The blank canvas stood tall and thin in front of Aya. Here, everything was at stake. Somehow, she had to harness the forces at bay.

It began a week ago, very early one morning, while she was at work in her studio. She was gazing, in the white light of early dawn, at a yet untouched metal block, mixing paints and turpentine, when she heard a knock at the door. She paused, for no one came to her this early in the day. She walked across the space to the door. She was about to open it, when she noticed on the floor a letter that apparently had been slipped beneath the door. How did the mailman, or courier, get into the house, and then upstairs? She picked up the letter and opened the door, but no one was there. She went to the window facing the street and thought she spotted a man in a dark felt hat and long coat turn the corner. A heavy mist clung to him, surrounding him. When he disappeared around the corner, the mist vanished with him. Aya's head ached and her vision swayed.

The letter was on gold-red paper, scented and sealed with red wax. The message itself was headed by a coat of arms: twins sitting on a high throne.

Dear Miss Aya Dane,

I have been observing your work for some time now and believe it could be a right addition to my collection. You know who I am, I assume. But before your work can be added to my collection, you must pass a final adjudication. Forty days from the time you receive this letter, I wish to see one piece of art, old or new. You may choose which one, and in which medium. The choice is yours. But it must be one that captures your essence. This will be your sole opportunity.

Until then, my deepest respect,
Ari

Who was this Ari? Why did he come to her? Why did he choose her? The more she puzzled over it, the more she began to believe that she had heard his name, had encountered him, before. She began searching for him in her library. She noticed that almost every art book or art history treatise had his name on the copy, although one had to look closely to notice it. If he had a last name, it was never referenced. And his name wasn't written in the same script as the other words. It was always the same, ancient-looking script as the one used in the letter she received. And it was in red. She then searched him on the internet. The search results also appeared in that archaic script, inscribed in deep, dark red, as though he occupied his own interstitial space in virtual reality.

Ari, she read, was a rainmaker in the art world. He was on the board of a great number of museums and auction houses. His art columns could propel an artist to fame, and—here the red script became darker, a burgundy, a purple, a rough violet—destroy another. He was a terrifying, fascinating and elusive patron.

Aya learned that Ari would deliver emblazoned letters to the artists he took an interest in. To be chosen by him was considered a precious gift. Ari was not just one of the greatest art critics and collectors in the world. He was a force of nature. He could turn the fate of art and artists, make and unmake careers and lives.

No one knew where he was from. His past was unknown. Some claimed he was Indian, of a Maharaja family, others that he was an Iranian Jew, still others that he was born in the poorest neighborhood of Lima before rising to success as the apprentice of an eccentric Peruvian art collector and millionaire, yet others that he was a woman posing as a man.

Ari could immortalize an artist's work. It was believed that the ones whose work he included in his collection would live on forever. It was rumored that his invitations were always preceded by such hand-delivered, old-fashioned letters summoning artists to create their signature works of art. He would then decide whether or not the artist deserved a place in his collection. Aya felt a great disquiet: why had she never heard of Ari before, and if she had—and this doubt burrowed into her mind, plagued her—how could she have forgotten about him?

At first, confused and frightened, she decided to ignore the letter. She put it in a drawer in the armoire and tried to push it out of her mind, which worked at first. But little by little, eerie dreams began to haunt her and strange sounds interrupted her sleep. She couldn't tell if the noises were real or if she was imagining them.

One night she stood up in bed, fighting the sudden backache and headache that had seized her, and stared at the armoire. She thought she saw, thought she heard the drawers shake and rattle. A gust of wind blew in, a drawer cracked open, and something slid onto the floor. She walked across the bedroom, stepped through the glass panel doors and into the studio. There on the floor, golden and red, lay Ari's letter. When she picked it up, it seemed to turn a warmer burgundy, a more intense purple.

Aya placed it on the nightstand by her bed. If it wasn't hidden, it couldn't play tricks on her. The next morning, she discovered the letter at the foot of her bed. She put it back on the nightstand. And every morning after that she discovered the letter at the foot of her bed. Every morning she would put it back on the nightstand. Her backache and headache worsened. The stabbing pain became unbearable, and she found that she could now barely leave her bed.

Finally, one morning, she picked up the letter and re-read it, slowly and carefully. As she did, the pain in her back and head began to ebb. She closed her eyes. After so many years alone, why should she refuse such a chance? After all, her work was at a tipping point. She was, as people in the industry said, an artist on the rise, on the brink of success, although she wasn't quite there yet. So many others, like her, ended up completely forgotten, their talent wasted, their promise subdued. Why should she refuse success when it came to her door? She had worked hard to achieve what she had. Why not play by the rules, for once, play their game, *his* game, and show what she could do. Why not submit?

As these thoughts ran through Aya's mind, the pain subsided and a gentle calm swept over her. She would give Ari what he came looking for. And give herself the solace that evaded her.

five

Aya stood quietly in front of the canvas. Before she touched a new canvas, she always became consumed by fear and hope. A canvas or installation could become many things as a work progressed. Then the many would become the one, the canvas would submit to her, a perfect expression of her intentions, her desires for it, her dreams for herself. But a work could also turn hostile and reject her desire and touch, her labor. Worse yet, it could remain cut off from her, lifeless, unresponsive.

In the next few weeks, from its marked surface, Aya needed to produce her most accomplished work. She had fought hard for what she had, kept hope alive at the greatest cost. Here she was now, at the door of greatness. She could live on forever, despite and beyond society's desire to crush her, or simply forget her. No one could ever deny that she too had once existed, that she too had once lived. And, perhaps, the darkness would finally make its peace with her.

Aya wanted to break with her usual way of creating a work, to take a risk. Though her canvases could be seen as only a part of her installations, they were their heart, from which the colors and shapes found their expression in various materials—scratch and debris, wood, steel and, the most beautiful and elusive of all, glass. The colors and shapes themselves chose the material that fitted their own nature, and purpose. And always, on the lower right side, the slanted, broken porcelain red flower.

These installations, that had attracted art critics and buyers alike for their wild use of color and texture, were all at once chaotic, bewilderingly foreign and poignantly intimate. They were, for those who thought they knew how to look, touch and feel, a window into Aya's soul, otherwise guarded and occluded. Or so they said. In truth, they couldn't see her soul, for if they did, they would look away in horror and cover her work in a shroud. For her soul would speak of shards of glass, of wars fought and lost, of children adrift at sea and silent homes, of howls that cut through the night. It would speak of dystopias and fires, of bloodied roses and twisted branches.

This time, she would do things differently. It would be just the canvas. She would paint the canvas and it would be the origin and the final form.

She loosened her fingers, raised them to the sunlight and let the golden warmth filter through. She mixed the browns and blacks, the purples and yellows, and let the brush stroke the crisp surface. She added in a splash of blue and a hint of yellow. She plunged in, feeling off balance as she always did when she first began, never knowing exactly what would become of it, how the thoughts, feelings, flashes of color that haunted her would translate into matter. At first resistant, the canvas began to submit to the brush strokes and open up to the colors transforming it.

She lowered her arm and curved her wrist. The acts became more intimate, softer and deeper. Her body was no longer her own. It was obeying its own impulses, responding to its own mechanisms. She worked late into the night, letting the brushes guide her, and the darkness fall over her.

Hours later, when even the owls and other late-night creatures grew silent, she thought she heard a click, a snap. The sound was immediately followed by an acute headache and a burning pain in her chest. She put down the brushes and held her head in her hands until the pain subsided. She had pushed her mind and body to the limit.

The next morning, she woke up to the sound of her cell phone ringing. It was a blocked ID. She put it on silent. There was something intrusive about a caller who didn't want to reveal himself. Intrusive, willful, manipulative. Five minutes later, the phone rang again. And again, it was a blocked ID. Aya stared at the phone for a long time, then finally picked it up.

"Yes."

"Aya?"

She froze at the cold, male voice she knew so well and had fought so hard to forget.

"Please. Don't hang up."

That voice, that *voice*. It came at her like a herd of wild horses, rushed at her like a mad warrior from the barren steppes. As it always had.

"What do you want?"

"It's been fifteen years."

Aya closed her eyes.

"I need to see you, Aya."

"I thought you were dead. They all said you were dead..."

"They're all liars. Don't you see that yet? I'll be in Boston next week. Please. I've changed. Things have changed."

"I need time...Give me time."

She could feel his anger through the electric distance. She knew him so well. She could sense his struggle as he tried to control his rage. It had always gotten the best of him, and she was certain he would lose control once again. But in an even quieter, deeper voice, he finally said, "Yes, Aya. Anything you want. I'll call you in a week. Will see you in a week. I can't stay long."

And only then did he hang up, a little too fast, after a brief pause. Only someone who knew him as well as Aya did could sense the contained anger in the hurried gesture.

———

The bed sheets gathered her to them. The ceiling held her gaze. Aya tried to erase the sound of his voice in her head, of his memory and of the brutality behind it. But the same ache as earlier, albeit more intrusive, more vicious, tore through her, pinching her nerves and exploding through her eyes, down her head and neck. Memories rose from further back, beyond the violence at the surface, beyond the loneliness of exile, of when she was a little girl in her parents' home in Tangiers.

six

When she was a child, Aya's mother would wake her up with a kiss on the forehead and a soft "good morning" whispered in her ear. She would wake her up before the brother and the father, so Aya could help her set up the breakfast table, clean the kitchen, mop the floor. Aya enjoyed these moments she spent with her mother, in the quiet of early morning, with a popular Arab musician, a Sevillana or even Bach playing on the radio set to low. Her mother had been a music teacher in a private secondary school before having her two children, and playing different kinds of music in the morning was perhaps her way of remembering her life as it once was, or of telling herself that all wasn't forgotten. After completing the morning chores, Aya would dress, wash her face and tie her hair in a ponytail. Only then did the mother wake the father and brother up.

The warm smell of bread and fried eggs rose from the kitchen. She spread cheese and strawberry jam on the toasted baguette and cut the fried egg in the middle, to see the yellow spill over the white. She drank the freshly squeezed orange juice her mother had placed in front of her and watched as her mother heated the water and made two cups of strong, black coffee. A man entered the kitchen. He was tall and broad-shouldered. His skin was a light golden brown. His hair was thick and turning white at the temples. He was kind. He ruffled Aya's hair, winked at her and went to her mother. When he was younger, he looked like a movie star. No one would have guessed that he was an accountant in a dusty state-owned corporation with a circular future and little vanity. As the years passed, his singular charm faded, his eyes and his suit turned gray, and passersby stopped turning in their tracks to stare. But not for Aya. He was her father.

Her father held her mother in his arms and kissed her a long, deep kiss. "My love," he said to her in Arabic, their language of sensuousness. He let go of her and turned to look at the breakfast table where Aya was sitting, quietly eating her butter and honey toast, embarrassed at their demonstrations of love. Money was tight in Aya's household. The months when they had a little extra for outings or gifts were rare and few but the lack of money did not bear too harshly on them at first. Their apartment walls were covered in shelves of books. Aya's parents believed in what books said to them and were soothed and nourished by the elevated ideas they contained. In the beginning. But passing time and empty pockets soon took their toll on them.

There was frustration in her father's voice when he next spoke. Pointing at the chair next to Aya, he asked:

"Where is he?"

The mother crossed her arms over her chest and looked him straight in the eye.

"Asleep."

"Asleep? Wake him up. It's time to go."

She held his gaze, then answered with a tinge of defiance.

"He's awake."

"What's he doing, then?"

The mother's silence filled the room. Finally, she told him.

"You know how he gets. It's one of those days."

"He's praying again, isn't he."

"Well, it's a daily affair. Five times a day, they say. No day off."

Ignoring her sarcasm:

"Praying? He has an international coach coming to see him play! A future to prepare for! This is his last chance, after everything…Someone that talented, he can't just waste his life away."

"It's just a phase. You know how kids are these days. Don't fight it, it could get worse. Be patient with him, it will pass."

"The Qur'an blasting from his room the minute he comes home from school or from wherever he is. The beard, the prayer carpet in the middle of *our* living room. One day, he'll tell you how to dress and will want his sister out of school."

"Not in my house. He would never dare."

"Bring him to me. I want to hear him read that bloody book. You're shocked at my words? It *is* a bloody book…The likes of him bloodied it with their crimes."

"Don't say such ignorant things."

"That boy of yours can't even read his Arabic manuals properly, let alone the Qur'an. Bring him to me. I want him to *read* it to me."

"Let him be. It will pass, you'll see. I know my son."

"This is the same child who smoked cigarettes at twelve and drank my wine at sixteen. And God only knows what he did with girls. Just last summer, that dirty business we had to take care of for him. The dishonor. Our shame…"

"He's too intelligent for his own good. Too rebellious."

"And he will fail at everything. The world does not forgive that kind of spirit."

Her father sighed. He looked tired all of a sudden, tired and helpless, a sadness knotting his throat. Aya's father never spoke of religion. They never discussed religion at their house. He never said whether or not he believed in god, and refused to answer any question on the subject. "What is it to you, what is it to the world if I believe or do not believe?"

As Aya followed her father out the door, she heard her mother whisper, "My beautiful son." She closed her eyes and when opening them saw Aya looking at her, she smiled and added in a low voice, "*You* understand, don't you? You always understand everything." And Aya remembered how the lightness, suddenly, had given way to the heaviness of unuttered anger.

———

Aya was the odd one in her family. Whereas her family was tall and light and strong, like the people in the north of Morocco tend to be, descendants of the Visigoths, some say, she was thin, frail, with curly black hair that stood on end, resistant to every brush, even the round plastic ones made specifically for hair like hers, and brown skin that sometimes glowed golden in the sun. Her parents had often worried about her ability to adapt and fight back. But as she grew up, they realized she had an unflinching will and a steely resilience. Aya would hold her ground until they thought she would break, but she never did.

Aya didn't have any friends. She was a lonely child. Being around other people, having their eyes on her, whispering, laughing at her, was unbearable. There was no filter between them and her. She sensed everything they thought and felt about her, even the unspeakable things they wouldn't say. Being around others was painful and she preferred to stay alone. This choice, which wasn't a choice, incomprehensible to most, was met with anger and hatred. One day at lunchtime, she was cornered in the bathroom by a group of girls. One of them, a big, sloppy girl whose father was a feared, well-connected government official, dropped her books on the ground in front of Aya and told her to get on her knees and pick them up. Aya refused.

"You think you're better than everyone else. We'll show you."

Her friends pushed Aya to her knees, and again the big girl, who was their leader, told her to pick them up. Again, she said no. They kicked her and started booing. Aya just stared at the girl, without answering, without budging. She could see confusion, suspicion and then fear enter the girl's eyes. The fear mingled with hatred. Aya wondered whether they would kill her, and whether she would die, unnoticed, in a dirty corner of a poor schoolgirls' bathroom.

The bell rang and they backed off. The big girl spat on the ground and hissed, "Weirdo." And still Aya didn't say a word and didn't take her eyes off the girl. The bell rang again and Aya stayed where she was, quiet and unflinching. They turned and ran away. They never bothered her after that. Instead they began to avoid her, to change lanes to be far from her. They feared her like villagers fear the monstrous creatures beyond their walls. And the whispers and incessant gossip about her only increased and filled her head with their noise.

What they didn't know was that Aya had retreated inside her body, in the dark corners of her body, in the half-closed shell that had been preparing for her return, all this time, preparing to comfort her and soothe her.

That was around the time the schoolgirls and their teachers began to notice that whatever she did, she did well. And the hatred and rejection worsened. Except for one person.

The mathematics teacher was a veiled, religious woman. Her name was Miss Mai, which means water in Arabic. She was, and this was rare in the school Aya attended, a fair woman. Aya rarely spoke up in class, for she had incurred teachers' wrath in the past; they thought her correct answers were arrogant and a sign that Aya believed she was superior to them. They never missed a chance to make fun of her in the classroom, or ignore her, or punish her, for her knowledge of their subject often surpassed theirs. She had opted, therefore, for silence.

Then one year, the year she turned fourteen, a new math teacher came to the school. Miss Mai had, it was whispered, been trained in Damascus, before the war. She had also, and this was perhaps untrue, been to Iran. She admired the Iranians, the strength of their public schools, geared toward math and science, and their unwavering commitment to the nation and to God. She had been told about Aya, about her arrogance and immodesty, and so Aya braced for another year of silence and rejection. The new teacher tested her students on the first day of class.

Miss Mai returned Aya's copy to her with a quizzical expression on her face. She tested them again the next day, and again, she returned Aya's copy to her, in silence, but with, Aya thought, some gentleness. Then on the third day, she gave out a third test, but only to Aya. Miss Mai then called Aya to her desk and, a half-smile illuminating her otherwise dark, austere face, she said, "Tell me about this work, Miss Dane." Aya kept her eyes lowered and her mouth shut. "Do you know what it is you just did?" Aya knew what was coming. She extended her hands, her fingers pressed against each other, to form a soft curve, which teachers would then hit with the back of a ruler, as hard as they could. Miss Mai looked at Aya's hands, in surprise, then put her hands above hers and pressed them down. "No, you don't understand. This isn't a punishment. I called you here because this," she pointed to Aya's copy lying on her desk, "is remarkable. You know things, instinctively it seems, that you shouldn't know at your age, that you shouldn't even know in high school. And I don't know how to explain that."

Aya looked into her eyes, saw no malice or hatred there. "Neither can I," Aya whispered.

Miss Mai was quiet and seemed to hesitate. "You are talented, incredibly so. I'll give you that. But talent is a trap, it's from the devil. It can make you arrogant and lazy. It can lead you down the path of self-doubt and self destruction. It's a curse. Your true gift is grit. You are brave. That's what God gave you," she told Aya. "That is the greatest quality a girl in our part of the world can have. But hide it well, make it seem unimportant, or they will crush you." When she saw the perplexed look in Aya's eyes, the teacher, usually hard and closed to her pupils, took Aya's face in her hands and said to her, "I can only help you for a while. I can only be there so far. This is my advice to you. Work hard, keep your eyes lowered. Then leave this country. Find a way. Swim across the blue channel if you must. Go. Run as far as you can from here. Don't ever look back. There is nothing left here. We are all just waiting for death."

Aya nodded and noticed the teacher's hands were still on hers, warm and comforting. It was the first time anyone at school had shown Aya kindness. And yet, that day, Aya knew something invaluable had been taken from her. She knew that the country she was born in wasn't intended for the likes of her. That she wasn't welcome there, that she would never be wanted there. The outside world and its constant, illogical succession of images, chopped and fragmented, would be a part of her forever.

seven

Aya pushed the swirling images and words back into their past, undressed and stepped into the shower. Her eyes were wide open and her body burned. The cold water soothed the searing heat that coursed through her.

She had changed from when she was a mousy little girl and a bony teen. Now in her mid-thirties, she was still small and thin. But her curly black hair was streaked with flashes of silvery white, and her large hazel eyes pressed against the golden brown of her skin. "An enigma, a wild charisma," David would say, as he gazed on her in the quiet of her home. Though she might go unnoticed in a street of tall, blonde women, once a glance set on her, on the peculiarity of her, it wouldn't be able to tear itself away.

After showering, Aya spent the day in her studio. While the living area of the apartment was cluttered, dark and filled with dusty objects, the work space was bare, except for her supplies and artworks, and for the light that flooded in during the high hours of day. Its only colors lay in the pigments she poured into her canvases. And this canvas, for Ari, was drawing her to it in new ways.

In working on her installations, she had found a way to control the composition process. While colors took on lives of their own and brushstrokes traced the granulated surfaces of canvases following their own impulses, pouring into other media, still she was able to guide it all, relinquishing control only at specific moments. But with this project, she sensed the opposite happening. It was taking hold, controlling *her*. She was losing her power over it. And yet, she had never felt such a rush of adrenaline, such a burning flow of energy. It was feeding into a deep, old hunger that she had forgotten she had.

———

Aya could have done, or been, many things. Her teachers had laid down their weapons to her will to succeed. The headmistress herself, a stark, harsh woman who had given her life to the responsibility of crushing individual freedom and ambition in her female students, finally gave up on Aya. "To be a wife and mother. That is why God put women on this earth. But if you must, choose something reasonable, valuable to our religion. Become a doctor, a mathematician, an engineer—something useful, honorable. No nonsense profession. And hope someone notices you."

Though deep down, Aya yearned for something else, she steeled herself with obedience and followed the headmistress's advice. She repressed her desire for color, texture, words, for the carnal beauty of unknown steppes and unplanned adventure, and instead found clarity and purpose in the hard sciences.

She received a scholarship to study at a prestigious university in America, renowned for science and math, in Cambridge, Massachusetts. There she studied math and physics, and honed her skills, while her natural abilities surged forth. Her research projects were deemed beautiful, and her findings elegant and precise. In this arena of pitiless competition, she didn't go unnoticed, and her future seemed a clean, linear path to excellence.

Then one day, shortly before she completed her studies, she went for a stroll and passed by an old Cambridge bookshop. It was a familiar route, one that she took whenever she preferred the long way home. She'd seen this bookshop many times in the past but had never ventured inside. As she was passing in front of the store, the door opened and an elderly woman stepped out. The old woman looked at Aya and held the door open, pointing inside. Aya glanced through the open door and noticed, lying on the carpeted floor of the otherwise impeccably kept store, a book with a worn blue cover. She turned toward the old woman, but she was gone. Aya felt as though she had known that woman her entire life, and she felt a pang of loss.

Aya entered the store, walked over to the book, bent down and peered at it. It was an art book from the 1940s. She picked it up and could smell the dust and ages rising from its closed pages. Opening it, she gazed in silence at the page.

It displayed the image of a painting: Two women, different yet eerily similar, shared a seat holding hands. Aya couldn't tell if they were the same woman. One was dressed like a European, and her heart was exposed, while the other was dressed in Mexican garb, and her heart looked red and strong. They shared a vein that emptied one heart to fill the other. She read the painting's title, *The Two Fridas*, and the name of the artist, unknown to her then, Frida Kahlo. Aya understood that the two women were in fact one and the same, that they were both Frida.

She held her breath, let her fingers roam over the image's bright colors and clinical demonstration of pain, felt the painting's clamor, its hunger, its power and irony. The painting's intricate, intertwined vulnerability and quiet suffering touched her heart in ways mathematics and physics did not. She saw her soul mirrored in the Mexican artist's work. The painting emerged as from the past, out of the traces of other paintings, other stunted mirrors.

Aya's feelings, lush and carnal, burst forth. She tingled with the power of presence and the discovery of pleasure. She felt formidably alive, her feet grounded, her blood pumping furiously through her veins, her spirit reawakened. She understood, at last, that there was a path that could lead her, perhaps not to happiness, but at least to an acceptance of herself. She used to think she was the strangest person in the world. And here was Frida Kahlo, someone strange like her.

At that moment she glimpsed her desired future, one unlike anything she had imagined or prepared for. This was what she was meant to be, what she needed to be—a painter, an artist whose work could bridge divided, opposing seas and redraw a downtrodden existence. And in what to others appeared a senseless, impulsive move, she changed the course of her life.

———

She started painting and drawing again, as she had as a child, but this time it was different, it was with purpose and clarity of will. And for the first time in her adult life, she felt at peace with work. Painting and drawing came naturally to Aya. She had always drawn but never valued it. It was not, as her school director would have said, "a useful act."

When Aya was younger, she would draw on rundown walls, bench corners, empty sidewalks and loose pieces of paper. She would bend the papers, displace a brick, add a flower to a bench and see it transformed. It had been an accessory, an instinctive, unnoticed habit throughout her life. She had never trusted it because she had been taught it was futile, useless, infantile, immoral. Her headmistress's models were the Iranian women nuclear scientists and medical doctors. Everything that was not science or math was a godless endeavor that fed on pride and self-indulgence. It was following the red-lipped devil down the path to hell. Though a woman's place was in the home—by her husband, her children and her bedroom prayer carpet, to sate, serve and obey—again, if she must, let her be an engineer or a doctor. Let her be of use.

Aya discovered the thrill of pleasurable work: layer after layer, she uncovered the subject that lay hidden in the canvas, in the stone. The act of creation was a riddle she must solve, a conversation she must have, a secret she must reveal. Her dedication to her craft became relentless, obsessive. Everything else in her life became secondary. Little did it matter if recognition came slowly or at great cost. Little did it matter that evil tongues whispered behind her back that her work seemed primitive, unimaginative, inappropriate. She chose not to listen.

She became driven by that shameless confidence she had recognized in Kahlo. She needed to break with the past, with the mousy little Tangiers girl starved for attention. She needed to mend and to heal, to repair a schism within herself. She felt akin to the anonymous Sumerian artisan who sculpted and painted the large-eyed, unblinking statues of Mesopotamia. Aya was, in fact, both the sculptor and the large-eyed Mesopotamian statue. Her gaze was unusual, noticing details with excruciating precision. She would take in every movement, every color, every variation or gradation in the scenes around her. Her eyes didn't filter the world as eyes should. They were like the unblinking orbs of the statues of Mesopotamia.

She wanted to feel, to be close to something, to touch the wet paint on canvas and believe that she belonged some-where, even if it was ephemeral. She wanted to paint the strangeness of being her to the world, inspired by a burgeon-ing need to claim a territory as her own.

And so, she changed paths. She quit her engineering program and applied to art school. There she hoped to find a sense of belonging, acceptance, but instead she felt more isolated than ever before. Despite her isolation, peers and teachers noticed her work and encouraged her to exhibit. Very soon, due to a rare mix of chance and talent, and the alignment of the stars, her work was exhibited, then picked up by the Museum of Modern Art in New York, the British Tate, and the Museum of Art, Architecture and Technology in Lisbon, the latest born of the contemporary art museums.

There was a haunting quality to her work, both unusual and familiar, repulsive and attractive, which drew people in. In her installations, her use of materials and debris mingled with a soft, sensuous use of color and of domestic scenes, creating an aching phantasmagoria, a metallic vulnerability. Hers was the expression of a broken machinery, a fragment-ed body split between two shores, two realities, two ways of being that, in the end, crumbled into tiny pieces that shat-tered all sense of identity. Everything was broken, except for the redness of the flower, the purple of the bougainvillea, the deep blue of the sea, all of which extended here and there, crisscrossed by wild winds and starry nebulas.

Art critics and collectors began to identify her, to make connections, to pin her to their words. "Exiled between East and West, between liberation and imprisonment, between the modern and the old," they said, "Aya Dane's canvases explore pain and courage at their most carnal. They are a relentless surge into the deepest fears of the colonized soul yearning for wholeness, of the Arab woman searching for her self." These words, both high praise and death sentences, filled Aya with despair. Instead of giving her pride, they intensified the constant noise in her head, the internal fury and relentless chatter that clanged inside her skull.

The more others praised and defined her, the more estranged Aya became, and the more estranged she became, the more interested they became in her work, Her sudden success had engendered its own bitterness. Instead of the love and acceptance Aya may have secretly yearned for, she began to receive degrading, hate-filled messages from anonymous senders, confronting her once again with a violence she thought she had left behind, in her native Tangiers. It was a different violence, perhaps, but one equally degrading and destructive; the type of verbal violence that so quickly descends into physical brutality and the hunt for prey.

She never did find out who sent her the messages. She was told to ignore them, to think of them as the price to pay for her sudden rise. But Aya knew these weren't words of mere envy or jealousy. They were ones of anger, hatred, confusion. They were the scorn of the migrant, the distrust of the foreigner, the fear of she who is different. They were the blind attacks of those who feel wholesome, pure, superior, but who know they are not. Who believe they once had been, until it was taken from them, and it's only a matter of time before they are whole, pure, superior once more. If only people like her remained at the gates, beyond the walls, out of mind, out of sight, inconsequential and easily painted over.

And so, as Aya's success grew, so did some people's vicious reactions to her and to her work, and so, also, did her own natural, homegrown distrust of the world. Like a clock whose mechanism begins to slow down and whose tick-tock begins to falter, she took a step back and closed the door to the outside world and its bustle. Aya herself didn't know why she was closing all doors to the world. The need for aloneness, for invisibility, was not something she could control. By the time Ari's invitation reached her, her break from the world was almost complete and other yearnings had begun to emerge.

The sun was setting and the glass panels began to shine in the twilight, projecting changing lights and shades onto the canvas. She stopped and put down the brushes. Only then did she notice that her shirt was cold and wet from sweat that had trickled down her spine and settled in the small of her back. Her head, left and right, and front and back, gave her an intense pain. She looked at the image that was forming on the canvas. The tension and anxiety ebbed, for the first time in days.

She opened the window, and the pale, crystalline rays of the setting December sun played on her skin. Her heart beat faster and her wet shirt draped itself around her like a suffocating sheet. The room soon became as cold as ice.

She quickly closed the window and stepped away from the canvas. An unexplainable, unutterable sadness took hold of her. It echoed through her, deadening everything in its wake. Then, an acute pain coursed through her, cut through her eyes and down her spine, and left her lying on the floor, unable to move or catch her breath.

eight

It was early in the summer and Aya was a young girl, running on the cobbled, hilly streets of Tangiers. Tangiers, the mythical blue-and-white city that sparkled on the southern shores of the Mediterranean. Tangiers, the crossroads between north and south, where the Mediterranean Sea met, but never mixed with, the Atlantic Ocean. Tangiers, one-time home to Western literary luminaries like Paul Bowles, William S. Burroughs and Gore Vidal or heiresses like Barbara Hutton. A Tangiers of lightness and gaiety, a Tangiers she had never known and that had not been created for the likes of her.

She had heard stories of these wealthy eccentrics who, in the 1940s and '50s, had built a reputation for Tangiers as one of the most sophisticated, glamorous cities in the world. Aya had never believed these stories, as her Tangiers was barred from the elegance, wealth and freedom of this old Tangiers. Her mother and father once talked about this bygone era, but added, with a mysterious sparkle in their eyes, that they never knew whether it had truly existed, for high hills and iron gates kept it secret. Perhaps, her mother suggested with a smile, Aya could one day find out for herself.

And one day, when the headmistress was having a better

day than usual, and when the heat was more unbearable than usual, the students were let off early and told to enjoy their free day in the half-cool of their homes, or in the verdant, early summer shade of the trees lining the promenade.

Aya wandered the city, taking in the sun and the slowness of the day. She stopped at a sweets and snacks stand and, for a mere two dirhams, bought a newspaper cone filled with sweetened, roasted peanuts. After having spent half her fortune on one of these delightful treats, she walked along happily enough, tasting the warm, sweet peanuts slowly, one by one.

Her wandering steps led her to a part of the city she had never been to, that she didn't even know still existed. Winding, cobbled streets circled lazily up hills of white-and-blue houses. Tangerine and lemon trees could be seen above the high walls, and purple and white bougainvillea curled up the bronze portals—the same flowers that, like carnal ghosts, would later inhabit her drawings.

This must be it, her heart pounded. This was the Tangiers of her parents' dreams. *It's real! I must tell Mother I found it, all by myself,* Aya thought excitedly. She took in the colors, the hues of orange, purple and yellow, the mosaics that appeared through the foliage, the blue of the Mediterranean Sea, as it contrasted with the pure white of the colonial walls. She was filled to the brim with emotion and a desire to explore. Aya's heart swelled with a furious joy that she would not feel again for many years.

As she was standing there, in awe, she heard a man yelling, and a dog barking ferociously. Startled, she looked around and saw a tall, light-haired man running toward her, his raised fist holding a stick, his other hand fastened around a leash. At the end of the leash was a terrifying German Shepherd. At first, all she could do was stare, frozen in place. She could hear the yelling and the barking, but she didn't know whom it was meant for. The words came to her as through a mist.

"Hey you, girl, get out! This is private property! Go back to your own neighborhood. Yes, you—Arab girl!"

Aya just stood there. She couldn't move or speak. She took in his singsong accent, the clipped way he spoke Arabic. Before he spoke, she thought he was of Tangiers, like her. But he wasn't, at least not like Aya was. He was foreign, perhaps one of those expats she had heard so much about. Here he was, as exotic as a white shark, and just as dangerous.

It took a while before Aya realized that the man was talking to *her*. That it was her presence in this secret Tangiers that he was denying. Slowly, she realized what had sparked his biting words and the barking dog's fury. It was the man's scorn—scorn for her worn clothing, her origins.

She stared at him, her eyes wide and afraid. The newspaper cone fell from her hands and the sweet, crisp peanuts fell on the brown cobbled streets.

Aya was not aware, until that instant, that she was a local. More precisely, she didn't know that expats, suave and chic, looked down on locals; they didn't want to mingle with them, or even be truly known by them.

The magic of the place disappeared, and Aya saw it as it was. Cold, unfeeling, arrogant. Or she saw herself as she was. Native, small, out of place. She stepped back, turned and ran home. She heard his clipped voice threaten her as she ran off, heard him say that it was time to build a wall against them, between them and us. Then he set his dog on her.

———

Aya never told anyone what happened on that rare, free day from school. She whispered it to her muñeca in the dark of her bed, in the folds of her arms, and made her promise never to tell. She lied about her injury. She said she fell on the jagged edge of a rock that plunged into the sea, that she almost fell onto the waiting black rocks below. She never lost the scar caused by the dog, a thin, angry red line that ran down the length of her calf.

She also never again smiled when her mother told her stories of the Tangiers of old, of eccentric expats and wealthy foreigners. That was the day Aya buried Tangiers' beauty and the dreamlike stories of its free, bygone years. That was also the day she understood that there was an "us" and a "them," and that she would always be one of the "them"—strange, cut off, written out of her own story. The day she realized that she had been born on the wrong side of the world.

nine

Working on the piece commissioned by Ari brought Aya back to the moment right before the tall foreigner and his dog chased her out of the Tangiers of secrets and took her innocence away, the moment that marked the end of her childhood.

Aya struggled against her fear. She tried to picture the colors of a perfect North African summer day—the warm sun of the Mediterranean on her skin, a red plastic ball on the golden sand, sweet pomegranate grains, and a vanilla and strawberry ice cream, sandwiched inside two wafers. But the brightness of the memory was blinding.

She slipped under the shower. The cold water was invigorating. She stepped out, poured a glass of water, took her pills. She got dressed: black pants, black shirt, flowery scarf around her shoulders. David would be there soon.

———

David was Boston born and bred. He was raised in the house built by his great-grandfather, as were his father and his grandfather before him. The Vandeer family never talked about how the great-grandfather had amassed, and kept, his wealth. Aya learned through David that his was one of America's most established and storied elites, an elite discreet and powerful, convinced of its own centrality, whose collective goal was the preservation of a way of life that had proven its resilience over generations.

And yet, he continued, pride mingling with unease, an elite that had engendered its own antagonists—religious reformers who questioned its wealth and how that wealth was put to use, philanthropists and pioneers of charitable organizations, social reformers, altruists and advocates working on behalf of the most vulnerable. David was of that lineage. Although trained at exercising power and defining others, he himself believed he could somehow make a difference. Though Aya did not have David's way with words and history, she told him that was perhaps precisely why and how his kind kept their power and status as generations came and went, as other elites came and went.

Aya was from another world. She came from a place where everything crumbled around you, except memories. She longed to have her own life, to call parts of her existence her own, to forge a path through the sand and into the granite. She aspired to a singular utopia, when she had been destined, by birth, to a silent fall into a surging dystopia. She knew that beyond her, beyond Aya Dane and her craft, nothing would remain, no children, no family, no grounded elite.

Their paths should never have crossed. Aya should perhaps never have fallen for him. But desire is a mystery. Perhaps it was their differences that pulled them to each other. Or perhaps it was because David was not what he seemed. He played by the rules, but only on the surface. He had a strong, square demeanor, but his blue eyes softened when he looked at her.

She thought he might be in finance, though she didn't

know for sure. He had had a golden childhood, but only in appearance, for his domestic family history was rough and brutal. David was a puzzle—smooth and golden, full of contradictions and questions. Aya, who had rarely connected with or been drawn to anyone in the past, felt drawn to him, understood by him, even. He would sit and listen to her, his hands crossed on his lap, and Aya felt she could tell him things that she had never told anyone before.

He sometimes wrote articles about American history and the immigrants that teemed to the country's shores. He had his theories about them, about her, about their work ethic and the country's diversity. He talked about empathy and openness, fundamental democratic values. But his theories about differences and immigrant struggles often included forays into mental illness and obscure neurological syndromes. Aya wondered why he wrote such things. The articles were intriguing—intriguing and, Aya thought, strange. The writing was convoluted and complex, especially for a man whose profession was wealth management. Strange, but interesting. Words on a page, she once told him, were what brought them together; words were what made them close, beyond the divide. Their apparent differences were a foil for their inability to ever fit totally into the roles they had been assigned at birth. A hunger for more, an insatiable curiosity for what lay on the other side, for the key to the keyless door, for what lay beneath the darkness, defined them.

———

David would ask about her when he arrived, ask if she'd taken her pills and gotten enough sleep. Then he would sit in his favorite chair and they would have their usual nighttime chats.

Aya wore the same outfit, every day. It was a habit of hers. Black pants and top, flat shoes and a wide, colorful scarf that hung loosely on her shoulders, covering the top of her body, that she wrapped around her hips when she was working. She outlined her eyes in gold to make them appear even wider and more golden than they already were. She rarely wore any jewelry, except for a small gold ring her mother had given her when she turned thirteen. The delicate ring, which she wore around her left thumb, was a family heirloom that had belonged to her grandmother and to her grandmother's mother before that, all tall, strong Mediterranean women like Aya's mother.

Waiting for David, she drank another glass of water. The pills made her mouth dry. The two of them rarely went out, rarely mixed with his friends, and Aya had none. She had met his friends in the past and didn't want to be around them. He understood. They were well-groomed, successful, sophisticated people. They had all the right diplomas, all the right names and all the right brands. They worked for all the right companies—those that didn't produce anything but speculated on everything. "We build dreams," "We change the world," "We impact," were their mantras. And, of course, they were in it for the long haul. They were an attractive group. Despite the variations in their skin color and slight differences here and there, they were a homogenous bunch, with similar goals. Ambition can do that, make diverse individuals crave the same thing, flattened by time: a respected existence within the fold, money, promotions, new property, perfect children, agelessness. And love—love that was always central to their conversations.

Love that pretended it was there, that it was unique and precious. But love that thrived on comparisons, that was always in competition with other loves, other lovers. Love that consumed itself and repressed real joy, real pleasure. Deep down, they were all the same, yearning for a love they did not know they had already lost. The difference between them and Aya was that she realized what she had lost.

Aya was their token foreigner—accomplished, talented, striking. Good enough to be with them. Being an Arab woman—which is what they saw her as, even though she didn't see herself as Arab, or American, or Muslim, didn't think of herself in those terms—was to be doubly foreign, both victim and foe. On some level, they viewed her with suspicion, she sensed. As though, despite all her efforts to be as American, as integrated as possible, they knew she was not. And they were right. She was from elsewhere, elsewhere altogether. And she belonged nowhere, and nowhere was what she wanted.

"When they looked at her," Aya asked David, "their hidden feelings as tangible and concrete as the painting that dripped from the canvas onto the floor, were they imagining her veil, dark and terrible beneath her skin, holding her wild hair in? Were they imagining the men from her land, dressed in black from black hood to black boots, hunting women like animals? Were they imagining the bloody warriors at their gates, come to take their wives and children? What lay beneath their words, in the interred dark—was it the monster of suspicion, the entrenched fear of the foreigner, the stranger, the other?"

And then there was that one question, the one that drove a wedge between Aya and David's friends, the one that made her decide never to see them again.

"Why don't you tell us about your parents, Aya. We're all friends, all from different places."

"Tell us about love. In the Middle East."

"Tell us how a man and a woman fall in love and stay in love in your part of the world."

Love.

———

Aya closed her eyes. She pushed the images away. Time had passed and David was late. Her head ached, the same acute pain she had felt the night before. Her eyes blurred and images faded. Darkness had come early for her this night.

ten

She was a little girl, once again, curled up on the couch in front of the smoky fireplace, feeling warm in the cold of a Tangiers winter. Books lined the fireplace and the white wooden shades were closed against the wind coming from the icy North. The apartment she lived in with her parents and her brother was a simple, almost drab, place. The only lavishness was the fireplace and the hundreds of books lining the walls. The TV was a ten-year-old model, and no one, except for Aya's brother Kareem who could watch it for hours on end and regularly complained that the image was blurry, ever bothered with it.

Aya held a book in her hands, her eyes glued to its pages. She had read it at least a hundred times. It was her favorite book, *The Diary of Anne Frank*. She only raised her eyes, as children sometimes do, to make sure her parents were nearby. And there they were, in the dimness of the afternoon, their arms around each other.

A song was playing. Aya remembered the brightness in her mother's eyes, her love of music, her passionate, almost childlike attachment to certain songs, as the song played on, and as her husband held her tightly against him. Leonard Cohen. "Dance Me to the End of Love."

They had forgotten that Aya was there, they had, it seemed, forgotten the whole world. They danced slowly in the bare living room. Aya breathed in her parents' love, crisp like an autumn afternoon, deep and quiet like a crystal lake in the reddening forest. And for a reason she could not understand then, forgotten thus, in the folds of all this tenderness, their dance made her feel safe and loved. They were letting her be, just as they were letting themselves be. It was their secret formula for their discreet happiness. For the rest of her life, Aya would yearn for that moment, for that enveloping sensuality; for the fullness of feeling she had known then, and that she would never know again. Love. Beyond the fleeting immediacy of joy, beyond the vulnerability of happiness. Love, held in the folds of a song.

A song that became *their* song, her parents' love song. The only love song in the world. The song the pianist was playing in the early hours of dawn only the day before. The song she had blocked out of her memory for over a decade, the song that was the reason she left David's apartment so abruptly, so early that holiday morning.

eleven

Aya looked at the man sitting beside her, his perfect profile and simple elegance. He returned her gaze, a quizzical expression in his eyes, quivering between concern and curiosity. He never quite managed to tear her away from the fantasy of their beginnings, from the fantasy that is every beginning. She could read her otherness in his eyes, taste her strangeness in his kiss, find annihilation in his touch. He asked her about her home, about her childhood, in peculiar ways, and thought carefully about her answers. He asked her about violence, asked if it was akin to the images seen on the screen. He asked her about sex, about women, about her violations, religiosity, sexuality, her femininity. He was interested in Islam, in her living of it and feeling of it.

David was of a rare breed, a cross between a latter-day Orientalist and an inextinguishable Don Quixote. Before David, Aya had only known two images of Islam—the unyielding image of Islam as vengeful fury, and the equally violent image of Islam as something to be feared and pushed away. These two opposing visions fed each other, mirrored each other, thrived on one another, but were poised to consume one another—radical, insatiable, monstrous.

These two images of the world, of her world—the one she had tried to leave behind, the one she didn't feel a belonging to and for which she felt only a nagging and disheartening nostalgia—was all she had known, until she met David. His view was an attempt to break the mold, to see the humanity, the suffering, the life beneath, to differ and consider. He was eager to understand those vast expanses of lands, peoples and nations that the media called "the Arab world," always prompt to decipher, hesitant to judge. He was intent on defending and healing a sickness that neither wanted nor knew how to be defended and healed.

But Aya wondered if he, like everyone else, wasn't trapped in a spiral of uncontainable images, caught in a reality where images had replaced facts, where the gaze had become frozen on the screen, blind to any other truth.

———

Aya and David had met at her final art exhibit, which David's girlfriend at the time, Catherine, insisted he accompany her to. "A talented, powerful artist from the East, who goes by the cryptic name of Aya Dane," she'd told him. "She never exposes herself. This is her first exhibit in five years, and I heard it would be her last. After tonight, she will disappear."

David's girlfriend, whom he had known since he was a child, and whose family had been sailing with his for years, was a professor of philosophy at a local liberal arts college. Catherine Dumont was tall and beautiful, of perfect stock and impeccable upbringing. She was raised in a wealthy suburb of Boston and had never spent much time in the city.

When she started living in the city, she came apart somewhat. She saw herself as a naïve provincial who needed exposure, and so exposure was what she went looking for.

She explored the ultra-urban, ethnic, seedy, marginal, decaying areas of town and turned her search into a furious quest for redemption sprung from the Anglican guilt she had been carrying all her life, and only now realized she had been carrying. But she needed David by her side to do so. And so, whenever she pushed open a new door in a new area of town, she insisted he come with her. That was how David walked into Aya's final exhibit.

Aya was standing off to one side, away from the crowd. She never stayed long, if she came at all, to her showings, and was about to leave. The gallery owner was explaining her work to people and the tumult of sounds, colors and movement pounded against her temples. At that moment, a tall, elegant man walked into the exhibit space. He kept the door open for the young woman who followed him in. They lingered at the doorway. They looked perfect together.

Aya felt a pang, an ache, something akin to longing. Her eyes caught the white gallery light and she raised her hand to shield them against it.

The man looked straight at her. His arms hung loosely at his side and his eyes were fixed on her. It seemed time no longer mattered to him. The woman next to him took him by the hand, and Aya watched as they walked toward her. Aya stood still and fought her desire to run. She was strangely attracted to the couple.

The woman was saying to her companion, "Come, don't miss this chance to meet her. She's an amazing artist. She expresses so much, the tragedies of her country and her family. Her work is overwhelming. Come, meet her."

A dark, shameful feeling flowed through Aya. It took precedence over her longing for their perfection, their beauty. It transformed her longing into envy and fed into the envy, giving it form and purpose.

She watched as they made their way to her through the crowd. She waited for them to reach her and then held out her hand to the woman. She smiled at them, her smile detached and unemotional. The woman took Aya's hand in hers and shook it warmly. Her blonde hair caught the light, and again Aya longed for her, longed to be her. She was already nostalgic for her.

The woman spoke first.

"Aya Dane, it's an honor to meet you. I'm Catherine Dumont and this is my fiancé, David Vandeer."

Catherine turned to David. Aya could see she was embarrassed and now slightly worried by his silence and his unusual awkwardness.

"Hello. I'm David."

"Aya."

Later on, when David became hers, Catherine called Aya. "I knew almost immediately," she began. "I knew I'd made a terrible mistake bringing David there, insisting he meet you. That moment, before even David knew, I realized I'd lost him. He broke my heart."

She hesitated, then started again. It was not like her to fabricate stories.

"That's not it. I pushed him into breaking my heart. I dragged him with me down a path that should have been mine only. I made it his obligation. And, finally, I opened the wrong door and David, though he'd never wanted it, found freedom. He found the incommensurable in your wide golden eyes and furious talent, Ms. Aya Dane. And to my own surprise," she added with a slight laugh, "I felt liberated, too. I no longer had to choose between my own hidden desire to experiment and the weight of generations of tradition. I don't know how long this feeling will last. All I know is that David is no longer mine and that I'm free."

Then she concluded,

"Keep him, he's yours. Though you'll soon tire of him, I predict."

When Aya left the gallery by the back door that night, she thought she saw Catherine and David in the shadows of an alleyway. The fog and cold rose around them, and their faces were in the dark, but their words rose crystal clear into the night. "There is a wildness in her, a *sickness*, you don't see it yet. One day, she will do to you what you did to me."

David answered, "It's not what you think it is. She's not what you think she is."

Then Aya heard footsteps behind her and the rest of their words faded into the night, as though a black bird had swallowed them whole.

twelve

For a time, Aya thought she would find peace with David. But David had demons of his own. He broke easily to her presence, because the cracks were already there. Reluctantly, he told her about his family, slowly, coolly, bit by bit, for that was the only way he knew how.

David's family was burdened with secrets and darkness that he bantered away in light talk. His sense of reserve chipped away at his emotions as they bubbled to the surface, filtering pain with detachment.

He had grown up in a household with a father always working and a mother who had quit her job to take care of him and his siblings. He was grateful for the long hours his father worked, but his mother's sacrifice he took for granted. The family enjoyed summer homes and European vacations. The kids attended exclusive boarding schools. There were summer sports and winter sports, fall festivities and spring champagne cocktails on the lawn. Their hydrangeas bloomed all colors, and their horses—which they kept at the country home—were purebreds.

David had been sent to boarding school very young, and there he learned to control his tears alone, in the dark, among strangers. While in boarding school, he was rarely invited home, except for major holidays—Thanksgiving, Christmas, Yom Kippur, though he didn't know why the school allowed him to return home for Yom Kippur, when he wasn't even Jewish. It was something his paternal grandmother, Beck Vandeer, insisted on. He would go to his grandmother's house for that holiday and stay with her in the grave silence of the candlelit card-room, one of the smallest in her house, where she liked most to spend Yom Kippur, reading a book in a language David had never heard before but that may have been Hebrew. Although he couldn't understand why his grandmother, the aristocratic Beck Vandeer, would be reading a book in Hebrew, or observing Yom Kippur.

Aya listened in silence while David told her his peculiar little stories that portrayed a childhood that was not one. They had that in common, a childhood eaten up by adults. But David had darker demons than those that sang of lovelessness, demons he didn't know were still there, lurking in the dark.

———

When summer hit the city and Boston's heat became stifling, David invited Aya to Martha's Vineyard and their family property, where his grandmother summered. Aya had never left Boston in the summer. She never left Boston because she was afraid of flying, of long car rides and trains. She was also afraid of leaving her work unattended. She imagined it vulnerable to any accident or break-in. A cat could enter through a half-open window or a ray of sun might burn through a yet unfinished canvas. She had said no, at first.

"You'll like my grandmother, she reminds me of you."

"She reminds you of me!"

An aristocratic old lady that reminded David of Aya Dane.

"Yes. Though I don't know why."

On the ferry crossing over, David told her about his grandfather. When his father was a child, David's grandfather would bring his mistresses home, traversing the sunroom where his wife was having tea with her friends. Very soon, the tea turned into ice martinis, and his grandmother's eyes glazed into distant hardness. She would pretend she didn't see him, and her friends—all women of her station—would whisper that perhaps Johnny Vandeer was the worst of them all. Beck Vandeer won some justice in the end, for her husband died before her and left her a vast estate that had allowed her to find pleasure and freedom of her own.

———

A car was waiting for David and Aya at Edgartown harbor. A simple, nondescript car, as everything seemed to be on Martha's Vineyard, where extreme wealth camouflaged behind lush gray-green trees and stone-gray homes. As they drove toward Beck Vandeer's estate, the blue-green of the ocean and the town's quaint, colorful façades painted a fairytale picture of the Vineyard. It was a series of gingerbread homes that the witches had abandoned to the children. Nevertheless, the chill, despite the high summer heat, was perceptible. They drove past the gingerbread homes and the pristine roads lining the shore. The water surrounded the land on all sides, the forest in the island's interior became dark and wild. David told Aya of the natives that once populated these shores, before the white settlers eradicated their tribes. That must be the darkness that Aya sensed beneath the soft-hued bacchanalias of crystalline privilege.

David explained that many of the stately homes had been built inside these very forests, their stairs lapping the brown sands and white waves.

The car stopped in front of a wooden barrier, the chauffeur descended and raised it. As the car drove past the raised barrier, they entered another world, a secret world, timeless, hushed. The wheels crushed the gravel covering the path, and a deep, dark silence engulfed them. Large, wrought-iron gates rose from the rugged stone wall that surrounded the property. They drove in and he parked the car in front of the understated, brick colonial house, whose columned veranda faced a lush garden and ancient pine trees.

When they stepped out of the car, a tall, blonde woman, followed by two large dogs, came toward them. Aya's heart beat faster and she was back in the Tangiers of secrets, where a blond, blue-eyed man and his German Shepherd chased her away from the cobbled high streets as if she were a stray cat. The woman had almost reached them. Only then did Aya see that she was elderly, her back frail, and the dogs at her side, very tame, very affectionate Golden Retrievers.

David's voice broke the silence.

"Nana Beck, this is Aya Dane. Aya, meet Beck Vandeer, my grandmother."

He was smiling, perfectly at ease, comfortably at home. He was different, somehow. The veneer of sophistication he carried in the city, here took on a more natural depth. He had returned to his habitat and was rooting himself fast into ground that had nurtured him.

Aya smiled and held out her hand to the elegant woman who was David's grandmother. Beck was Aya's opposite: tall, blonde, grand. Her grip was firm and warm. Later, Aya asked David how he could see anything in common between them. Anyone could see that they came from opposite worlds that were never supposed to meet.

Aya looked into Beck's eyes. Their bright blue color was

heightened by skin-tone foundation and golden eye shadow. They were the eyes of an upper-class woman accustomed to wealth and others' obedience.

Then Aya saw something else there. Something that surprised her, that should not be there, not in the eyes of a woman like Beck Vandeer. Aya saw sadness: a deep, immutable, unquenchable sadness.

The sadness Aya saw in David's grandmother's eyes was familiar to her. It was the sadness caused by men, by bullying, by callous disregard, by unspoken humiliation. It was a sadness Aya was so familiar with that she wanted to take the aristocratic older woman in her arms and whisper soothing words in Arabic in her ears: "*Oumi*, old mother, my sister, this too shall pass." The same words she had heard women of all generations say to each other, back there, in the home country. Words she knew to be universal, understood by a certain type of woman—the type who had lived inexpressible things— everywhere. But then she almost laughed at the absurdity of this thought. Beck Vandeer was the type to despise weakness and look down on her own pain.

Beck was the first, and only, person in David's life whom Aya felt a connection to. Though the older, bejeweled woman, who had sat at kings' and presidents' tables, at first barely spoke a word to her, Aya knew she was deeply aware of her presence and that her presence comforted her. She could feel the connection, the kindred spirit. She too was of the old country. The old country was wherever pain and loss simmer down to acceptance, to resilience, barely short of resistance and hope.

Aya sensed that the older woman liked her, even though no one else but David could see it, or if they did, could understand it.

In David's family, everyone thought Beck was a little off, not quite right in the head. David said to Aya, "Beck likes you, and she doesn't like anyone. She's a bit batty, though."

David's extended family was also there. His parents, siblings, aunts, uncles, cousins all came to spend a part of their summer in their family home. Aya tried to avoid them touching her or getting too close to her. They neither minded nor noticed. Aya remembered them as colors. When they passed near her, she saw flashes of color of various intensities and hues: violet for the aunt who smoked her Marlboro Reds and drank her vodka in secret; bright pink for the cousin who kept taking pictures of herself in the house and garden to post on her Instagram; orange for the young girl who twirled her brown hair as she spoke to you; gray and yellow for David's parents—she wafer thin, he always off on a most important phone call, even late into the night.

Were Aya to paint them all, it would be with—as its centerpieces—disharmony and addiction. Their world, strange as it were, smelled like hers, of naphthalene and methylated spirit, filled with nostalgia and burning regret. They roamed around the estate, she told David, like patients at a health cure.

They didn't mind having Aya there, as she tended to stay away from them and never pretended she was, or could be, one of them. Their world smelled like hers but was also its point of erasure.

A couple of days after their arrival, the family went out fishing, leaving only Beck and Aya in the house.

As they sat on the veranda, sipping martinis, the slightly shabby rose garden ahead and the blue sea beyond, Aya asked the question she had wanted to ask her ever since she had come to the Vineyard.

"Beck, is that your real name?"

"My name is Rebecca, but everyone calls me Beck."

"Rebecca is a beautiful name."

Beck put down the martini, and sat quietly for a while.

"My husband, Jonathan, preferred 'Beck.'"

"But you don't."

Aya glanced at Beck and saw her mouth twitch in a curious half-smile and her fingers curl up on the thin stem of the martini glass. Then, her voice very still, she said:

"We married at a time when my father-in-law was trying to make a...legitimate... name for himself. My own father was very rich, and the two became business partners. To strengthen their partnership and crush competition, they decided a true union was necessary. That is how Jonathan and I married. What my father hadn't realized was my husband's profound contempt for Jews. And, well, that was what I was. Rebecca, daughter of Shauna and David Yacov. Rebecca Yacov. That's my name. He forbade me from practicing my faith and from keeping my birth name. That was how Beck came to be. He also insisted, and I agreed, for he was capable of terrible brutality, like the robber barons of the times, that our children never know of their Jewish heritage. But that, you can be sure, was not the worst thing my husband John was capable of, or did."

"So David is a Daoud, after all."

Beck laughed. Her sharp laughter rose into the quiet of late afternoon like a bird suddenly set free.

"David. That was my one victory over my dead husband. I asked that he be called David, like my father, and not Jonathan, like his father and grandfather before him."

"And Jonathan agreed?"

"He did. His business wasn't doing well. Johnny, like many businessmen, was a superstitious man, afraid that his past would catch up with him and destroy everything that he had built. By honoring my wish, he was probably hoping to be in the good graces of both the Old and the New Testament gods. And so, for once in his life, the man I called my husband, dropped the "fourth" after his grandson's name, dropped Jonathan for David, and there you had it. A David came to us."

"David doesn't know?"

"No, he doesn't."

"Well, that explains why you insisted David celebrate Yom Kippur."

"Yes. Just him, my grandson."

"A mystery solved."

Beck laughed again and Aya noticed the crystalline notes of her laughter chafing at the edges. *They are right, her family is right. She is a little off, chipped, strange. Like me,* she thought. Aya took in her austere silver hair, her elegant beige-and-white outfit, her matching beige Chanel shoes. She looked at her pink nail polish and noticed that it was a bit too bright, not well tended to, broken at the edges, slightly vulgar, strange, like her laughter. Like her. She was not what she appeared to be. She was an unspoken dream come true, Aya's heart beat faster, a perfection.

"I'd like to draw you, Beck. Would you agree to that? To pose for me?"

The older woman was startled out of her reverie.

"Well, child. I certainly didn't expect that one. I'll be… But, yes, go ahead. Why not? You're a good artist, aren't you? And they say you're a wild one when it comes to your work."

"I don't do portraits, if that's what you mean. Well, not in the way people understand portraiture." *I do self-portraits disguised as art,* she thought. Self-portraits of pain and loss, of the golden light hidden beneath a darkened eyelid. In the way of the Norwegians, of the Mexicans, of all those who sit at their easel when their loved ones are taken from them. Aya looked at Beck and thought she saw her thin, prim mouth open in an all-engulfing scream. She took the older woman's hands in hers.

"Think of it as a token of my admiration, dear one."

"Then I agree. Think of it as me welcoming you to this damned place."

Aya nodded, Beck's cryptic words falling into her ears like the pieces of an incomplete puzzle.

Beck posed for Aya and she painted her every day, in the late afternoon when the family was on the boat or in the village or playing ball on the lawn, during that brief summer holiday, the only one Aya had ever had, at Beck's graying property on the Vineyard. When she finished and showed Beck the portrait, thin tears welled up in the older woman's eyes. Beck, whose cold veneer of puritan containment rarely left her, put a hand on Aya's.

"I am young here. I am...full of light?"

Aya nodded.

"I painted the courage of you, as I imagined you to be. As I knew you were. You are Rebecca Yacov again, not Beck, or Becky."

"I've had portraits done of me, in the past. But this is the only one I intend to honor as my own."

"It's yours. A gift."

"Not a parting gift, I hope?"

Aya was quiet. Beck continued.

"To imagine you will stay with my grandson is...not something I can see you doing. Pity, you could have saved each other."

They looked at each other, smiled, at ease with each other. They understood each other. In their world, it was always too late to be saved. Beck served herself another martini and downed it.

"We are the same, you and I, but everyone out there seems to have conveniently forgotten it. We're mutts, and they can't get rid of us, and God knows they've tried."

Aya admired the older woman's still beautiful, aquiline profile. She was moved at how much David looked like her. She was pleased for her that the grandson who carried her heritage, looked like her. Even if she left, he would be rooted in ways he could never imagine.

"Tell him, Beck. Before it's too late. Your husband is gone, even his ghost is gone. I can feel it. Tell David who he is."

"And you, who tells you who you are?"

Again, that edginess in her tone, the final, cackling, tone-deaf break in the sentence. I do, Aya wanted to retaliate. I tell myself my past, my present and my future. But it's new and it terrifies me. All those who could have told me my story or remembered alongside me have died or left. I am alone and conflicting images in my mind are smoothed into a narrative I control for now, or think I control. But instead, she answered.

"I peek into my paintings and see a glimpse of what I am."

Aya turned to face the wilted rose garden and the pine trees that lined the grounds.

Soon after their meeting, David's grandmother passed away. She was given a proper Anglican burial that Aya did not attend. Aya told David that was the final violation his family had done to Rebecca Yacov and that she could not bear to see it. He admitted to having recently found out about his grandmother's Hebraic faith but he also claimed that he didn't believe it mattered that much to the old woman. He said that she didn't mind, that she wanted to be buried with her husband, on the land where her children and grandchildren would also one day be buried. He added, "But she left you something in her will. She said she didn't want anyone else to have it. You should receive it by next week."

A couple of days later, Aya received a package. She knew what it was. It was a canvas. It was the portrait she had made of Beck only a few weeks earlier.

She held the cold, dusty canvas in her hands and took in the piercing blue eyes of an eternally youthful Beck Vandeer. Beck's affection for her, the connection they shared, the quietness that soothed their words and cradled their secrets, away from the crowd, was the only real love affair Aya had had in her life. And Aya, who was increasingly plagued by memories of her past and haunted by the fear of what was yet to come, held on to the physicality of canvas and painting.

This is real, she thought. *I'm not imagining it. No one can deny me this. A love returned. Thank you, Beck. You have moved me from the limbo of exile into the hopefulness of home.* For the first and last time in her life, Aya was in love.

thirteen

David's strong hand rested on hers. His hand was warm. And yet Aya was cold. She was often cold. But there were times when the cold was more intense, more trying than others. Like today. When the secrets confided to David collided with her desire to be left unknown.

Later that night, in the quiet of her apartment, David wanted to talk about her brother. He asked her, his clear blue eyes holding hers in their gaze.

"Your brother is really here? In Boston?"

"Yes, he is."

"What does he want?"

"To see me."

"Why don't you ever talk about him?"

"There's nothing to say. I left it, left *them*, all behind. My life is here now."

But that wasn't exactly true. For fifteen years, Aya had kept the past buried and never went digging for it. She didn't need to: it dug itself out. These past few weeks, the broken memories had resurfaced, triggered by the pianist's forlorn song, by Ari's invitation, or by her brother's call. She herself didn't know for certain.

For fifteen years, they had all disappeared. She never

wondered where they went, for their absence allowed her peace. When Aya tried to remember her childhood or her days as a girl in Tangiers, all she could conjure were various shades of faded colors and dim noises.

Lately, the memories started coming back to her, in fragments and in sparks. They simply began rising to the surface and, Aya had to admit to this, but softly, lest they think she had gone mad: they *spoke* to her. They did not have their own *presence*, of course, but they were separate from her. They were not the same as her. They had their own voice.

Now, her past haunted her, memories of her home pursued her. They were constantly with her, like wild wolves on the prowl, waiting to be hungry enough, or for her to be exhausted enough, to circle in. They lived there, inside her. They disturbed her daily routine and transformed the finest meals into ashes. They sneaked into bed with her and stole her sleep. As time passed, and instead of subsiding, the memories became more vivid and acute. They filled the darkness within, were the darkness within. When Aya left Tangiers, all those years ago, she thought she would leave the darkness behind. But, here they were, once again. They had followed her into her new life and there was no respite from it.

"What are so you afraid of, then? If it's all behind you, nothing can hurt you now."

"That's not it. You wouldn't understand."

"What are you hiding from me? Tell me."

"What is it you want to know?"

"Why haven't you ever said anything about your brother before?"

Aya was quiet. She had to be careful not to divulge too much. She wasn't sure how much she should tell him. These were her secrets: secrets that helped maintain the walls and keep the darkness at bay, secrets that nourished her work and breathed life into the inert canvas. What would happen if she told him everything?

"My brother is not a man you would want to meet. He strayed from the path."

David sat down in front of Aya. The large glass panels opening onto her studio gleamed softly behind him. He waited.

"I haven't seen Kareem in over fifteen years. I never thought he would find me, come looking for me."

"Are you frightened of him?"

"Yes. And you would be too, if you ever met him. That's why I can't see him."

"What happened? Tell me, Aya. I need to know. You need to say it."

Aya's gaze strayed to the glass panels, eager to have him gone for the night, to close the glass doors behind her and lose herself in the painting. Ari was waiting; she had to tone down her life to its bare minimum. And she couldn't tell David about her brother.

She felt dizzy. The room blurred and turned around her. The now familiar, cruel pain seared through her head and everything turned black.

fourteen

"Aya, Aya."

Aya woke up to David's drill-like repetition of her name.

Aya looked around her and realized that she was stretched out on the couch, and that sweat drenched her body. Images flooded her, unannounced, unhindered, hard like a brick wall falling on ice-cold water.

Aya could tell that David was worried, his fingers on his phone, hesitating to dial a number, to get help.

"Aya, these spells of yours, they may be more than you think they are."

"It's the work, the lack of sleep, of food."

"It could be something more."

He looked at her, steadily, trying to probe into her.

Aya opened her mouth but the dryness blocked the sound. She wanted to tell him, but couldn't. Then a thought came to her, popping up from the darkness like a Jack springing out of the box. It's because of a *secret*, unspeakable shame, buried under years of lies and self-neglect, which Aya couldn't utter or still fully remember.

"Aya, you need to talk to me. I need to understand. That's why I'm here."

"What do you wish to know? Doesn't what you already have from me satisfy you?"

"I need to know you more, to understand why you are this way. Why is that so suspicious to you?"

David's tone terrified her. There was an urgency to his words that hacked into her defenses and revealed his frustration and his exhaustion. Perhaps he had understood that fulfillment with her would always be illusory, a solitary project.

Aya looked at him and saw steel in his eyes and jaws. Where had the tenderness gone? Why had he taken it back? He held a hypodermic needle between his thumb and his middle fingers. It was a tranquilizing medication that one of his doctor friends had prescribed for him—people like David could get any kind of drug, any time—which he sometimes convinced her to take, "for her anxiety." He took her hand and turned her wrist, blue veins facing him, toward him. His hand holding hers was cold. He held her wrist, where the white skin meets the blue vein. He pressed the needle until it broke through the skin and into her vein, expertly, as though it were a gesture he was used to. An eerie calm soon submerged her. She felt better.

She had built a fortress, both within and around her. She was beginning to feel the walls fissuring, and some even giving way. Now she felt tired, drained of strength. Her back stooped slightly, like a woman who had aged too fast, who had seen her years slip away from her unchecked, like sand sliding down the desert dunes.

Would he choose to leave her? Would he leave her because she kept secrets from him? Aya thought she saw a blonde silhouette; that of an elegant, sophisticated woman, standing outside in the street, lit only by a street lamp. Was it Catherine, standing there in wait, for David to come down so that she might take him back to their world? Catherine had always known that David would be burnt by the wilderness inside Aya. She had been patient, smarter than she was, more in love than Aya thought her to be. Beyond cruelty and jealousy, a woman in wait for the man she loved.

Aya walked to the window, looked outside, her heart ready to tear, but there was no one there. Only high trees and bright yellow lights that lined the street. No fair-complexioned, blonde-haired woman was waiting for a man in the cold, dark street. The only human presence was Aya's emaciated face and enlarged eyes, reflected in the windowpane.

Aya breathed deeply, relieved and terrified all at once.

She wasn't a coward, but today she was afraid. She was afraid of a future without him, of the bleakness, the absence of warmth and love that surely lay ahead if she were to end it with him. She couldn't bring herself to do it.

David was her only remaining close, human connection, the only touch she could stand, the only body which did not stifle hers. She couldn't lose that as well, not after everything she had already lost, not at such an *important* time in her life.

She wasn't ready to face the darkness alone, not yet. She wasn't ready to give in to the flood demanding to be let in. She had erected a fortress between the world and her, and its fractures were getting deeper. She knew that letting David go would make her meticulously crafted defenses turn against her, devour her.

She needed to tell him something, a story he would believe, one he would love even, and that would make him stay with her a while longer.

And so Aya told David a tale, of monsters and ghosts.

fifteen

Kareem had fallen in with the wrong crowd when he was fifteen. Their neighborhood had changed gradually, over the years, but Kareem's change was sudden.

From a relaxed, bustling district with its small shops, Art Deco furniture stores, fresh fruit and fish stalls, it had fallen on hard times. Like the entire city of Tangiers, except for its gold-and-blue hillside quarters, untouched as ever by the misfortunes of the world, Aya's street had lost its luster, and its relative prosperity had vanished into thin air. Forgotten were the days when Tangiers could still sustain neighborhood life, while remaining open to the world. Forgotten were the promises of light-hearted exchanges, open kisses and moonlit poetry.

Now, families saw their children leave the country to try their luck under whiter skies. Now, homes were emptied of meaning and pride. Now, the tumbledown buildings were filled with West African refugees and migrants trying to reach Europe, while their landlords bled them dry for a hole in the wall.

Even the glistening blue of the Mediterranean Sea took on nightmarish hues of red and black, of drowned Zodiac boats carrying children. The greatest graveyard in the world, that's what the Mediterranean became for them. Between two lands, a grave. There was no beauty left in the sea. It had turned into an unquenchable monster, luring dreamers with false promises. For right there, clearly visible on clear days, was Spain—at arm's reach.

But do people ever learn? Hope can become so great, and despair so deep. The sea had become at once the most formidable fortress, and the lightest of obstacles. This paradox now ate away at Tangiers, depriving her children of sleep and food, emptying every day of its joy, turning fear into resolve.

And that was when Aya's brother became a man, that moment when her family's neighborhood finally slipped. Many of the neighborhood boys dropped out of school, joined the local religious gangs. Others joined the more profitable drug or immigration networks. But all these groups were linked by strong ties, ties that bind beneath the dark surface. Still other boys tried to leave, many failed, many left and returned only to leave again, and many remained in limbo, between here and there, lost and seeking refuge.

And the girls? They remained in school as long as they could. When they could, they would leave as well, or drop out and work in factories, or closed rooms. What were the options? But this is about the boys—brothers—and what happened to them. It's so difficult to build trust unless you fold as well. Unless you bend your head and accept the new laws that were written without you and against you. And the society they were building, Aya told David, had already excluded the likes of her.

She, Aya, was always the strange one, one of the few lucky ones, too few still to bend statistics their way or make a home, here or there, a more livable place. Tangiers had changed and left her on the margins to fend for herself.

Kareem had grown up with that change, he *was* that change in their street, their neighborhood, their frontier town. It must have been there, inside him, the decrepitude of the place. For no one changes suddenly, the signs are simply misread. It's the readers who want to be misled, to remain blind to the dangers all around, until it's too late. He joined the neighborhood mosque, despite her parents' plea to leave religion to grown-ups and concentrate instead on his studies, his football, his way out.

Her parents, adamantly secular, perhaps even atheist. They could not accept that their son had turned to religion for answers. They asked him if he had ever read the Qur'an, if he even understood it. And, in the end, they shrugged their shoulders. For this too shall pass, the young must rebel before growing up. Her parents. Apart from the love they once shared, they didn't understand much about the world.

One night, Aya's brother left. They couldn't find him anywhere. Her parents knocked on every door on their street, questioned the neighbors, especially those whose sons were part of Kareem's new crowd. But he was nowhere to be found.

A week later, he returned. Without a word of explanation, he came back home. But he was no longer the same Kareem. He had begun wearing a long beard and dressing in the long pants and shirt that Afghanis and Pakistanis are said to wear.

He didn't stay for long. A year later, he was gone again, and they never saw him again. Some said he left for Afghanistan, to fight the jihad. Others said he left for Europe but never made it across the sea. Her family never knew for certain, and from then on they lived with their doubts and grief. Aya hadn't heard from him until last week, when her phone rang.

Aya lowered her head. "There, now you know everything. My past, my shame, my brother who terrifies me and who is now here, in Boston."

David looked at her. He leaned over, touched her hand and lowered his head, as though joining her.

Aya felt like a fraud to his kindness. She was ashamed of her lies, of the folktale she had just told him. A trickle of sweat ran down her back and her neck began to hurt. The pain soon became unbearable and she took her head in her hands and pressed tightly. It became difficult for her to breathe or see clearly.

The pain, the coldness, the fog had become familiar to her. She couldn't tell for certain when they had started, but they were now a part of her and she didn't believe they would ever let her be.

Aya had told David a tale he could understand, a tale that wasn't really one at all. It was a fairy tale, a myth.

But what if it wasn't a complete falsehood? What if her lies held more truth than her memories? She'd told him a semblance of her brother's story to feel safe, to protect herself a little longer, to postpone the inevitable solitude that would come with David seeing through her. Yet speaking those words opened a window, aired out a room, threw light on shadows she didn't know existed.

Was the made-up story in fact the truth of her family's past and the source of the fear Kareem triggered in her? Did he indeed leave them, abandon them, for an unknown shore and an unknown life he was unprepared for? Did he succumb to the violence and extremism of the Afghani militia groups or did he instead go down in the depths of the sea, as he tried to cross over to Europe?

David stood up, uncertainly.

"Don't you find it strange, Aya, that after all this time, your brother is here?" His crystal blue eyes had darkened. "Isn't it peculiar that he's able to cross borders with such ease?"

"Mistakes are made. I told you, I don't know where he's been all these years. He could have been anywhere. He could have been here, in this country."

"How did he get your number? You refuse to be listed."

"Social networks…anyone can be found."

"You barely have a web presence."

"What are you saying?"

He rubbed his eyes wearily. David had a regulated life. He measured success by the degree of order in another person's life. His actions made sense to him and so must the actions of others around him. Except for Aya. Aya was his fool's trap, the chaos around which he created order and the woman for whom he wanted to clear a path ahead.

"I'm saying it may not be Kareem."

"Why do you say that?"

"You haven't seen him or heard his voice in over a decade. How can you be certain it was him?"

"It was him."

"If it is, then you don't know how he found you, and why. Maybe he's been lurking around for a while. He may have been following you for days, weeks."

"Even if he had been, who knows what goes on in the head of a man who hasn't seen his sister for so long?"

"He could be dangerous."

"Maybe it's a final request. Perhaps seeing him would unlock the darkness."

"Let me come with you, Aya."

"That wouldn't be wise."

"Aya, my mouth is dry. I need a drink."

Aya went to the cabinet. As she reached for the curved liquor glasses, her hand brushed against the slender tea glasses she usually hid behind larger glasses. She must have forgotten to hide them the previous night.

She hesitated. Her back was turned. She took out the chiseled black box in which she kept the ingredients for the tea. Gently, she took out the rounded teapot, the mint tea, the black tea, the sugar. She made the tea like her grandmother used to, like her mother had taught her to. She took out a tray, placed the two slender red-and-gold tea glasses in a half-moon on the tray and set the teapot in the middle, between the glasses.

She came back to the living room, poured two glasses of tea and offered one to David, holding it delicately between three fingers, as she had been taught to do when she was a girl.

"Rituals are what keep us sane," she repeated, as her grandmother used to.

David looked at the glass of liquid gold she was offering him, and shook his head.

"You're not giving me much to work with here. And it's Scotch for me. Double shot, no ice, please. No, wait. Please sit down. I'll do it myself."

Aya took the tea back into the kitchen, poured his glass of brown, smoldering water into the sink and watched the withered leaves disappear down the drain. She held the shimmering tea tray in her hands for a while longer, staring down at it.

She came to the simple conclusion that David had rejected her tea knowing full well what it meant to her, what lay cradled in her offering to him. He must have known, surely, that within the crooked, rounded teapot rested the kernel of Aya's hidden being, her live memory which babbled of home and honey, half-asleep, begging to remain at peace in the dregs, and yet secretly waiting for someone like him. He must have known, surely, that the tie between them, though strange and dark, was stronger than any golden-haired romance he could have had. He must have known that, behind her coldness to him, behind her pride, there lay her hope.

The brass tea tray Aya held in her hands began to dissolve. She felt cracks appear on the wall, heard the sound of crumbling cement, of tumbling stone. But the walls and stones stood strong. They held her in. She steadied her hands. And she listened to the beating, burning heart beneath.

She pushed the tray into the garbage bin beneath the sink and returned to the living room, taking only her own glass of tea. With a gesture of her hand, she indicated he could help himself to the Scotch, inside the cupboard near the fireplace, where it had been waiting for him, it seemed, all along.

David got up and took the bottle of Lagavulin from the wooden cupboard. He then went into the kitchen, looked for the glass and the ice. At least that's what she assumed he was doing, though David's back was turned and she couldn't see.

He was in front of the sink. She heard the water running. She imagined it falling cool and light on his outstretched hands. She could hear a sound like the one of plastic on a hard surface. She heard a bright, crystal sound, almost a tune, delicate and light. The sound, pure and sweet at first, was fast becoming unbearable. High-pitched, metallic, continuous. She closed her eyes, pressed her hands against the warm tea glass, hoping the jagged sound would go away.

She was restless. What was taking him so long? What was he doing at the sink? She wanted to go to him, ask him to explain. The unbearable sound finally stopped, and he came back into the living room. He sat in front of her, his legs crossed, his whiskey in his hand.

He looked at her. She couldn't tell what he was thinking. His mouth tightened and his clear blue eyes seemed to turn a dark purple. Was it love, or fear, or pity in those eyes? He put down his glass, moved closer to her. She sensed his gentleness. She could also now sense his hesitation, and sadness.

He touched her hair, wrapped his arms around her.

"Let me help you. Stay with me for a while. Let me take care of you, just for a while."

Thoughts whirled in Aya's head. She wanted to let go. No, it was a trap, he was trapping her. He thought she could be fooled by his kindness. He wanted to take her away, to lock her up. His help could be devastating. She didn't belong in his world. She didn't belong with him.

To her silence, he added:

"I can help you, Aya. Let me help you. I need to see and know what you are doing. To understand this."

"This?"

"Yes. I need to make sense of it."

Beneath the tenderness of his words appeared an iron will—to understand, control, dominate. It was a familiar will. One Aya had grown up with. An ill-disguised male will, an unquenchable hunger.

She recognized it and knew he couldn't defeat it, despite his best intentions. He could not kill this beast. It was in David's veins, his legacy from father to son—the hunger which could transform clear blue eyes into deep, dark pools, and softness into whitened steel. Aya deflected, her words an attempt at weakening the hold he claimed.

"I need my studio. I need to be in my studio."

"Keep your studio. Or get a new one. But stay with me."

She pushed him gently and answered.

"No."

He went pale and his fists clenched, with the blunt anger of those who believed they had a right over her. It was the anger in her brother's voice, the anger in the voice of men in distant Tangiers, of policemen, teachers, immigration officers, doctors, past lovers and one-night stands. She closed her eyes tightly, fighting the urge to ask him to leave.

sixteen

David was the first man Aya had a relationship with. She had had other men, but they came quickly and left just as fast. That's how she wanted it to be. She didn't know how to keep a man around for long. She couldn't stand his heavy body on her white sheets or his demands as soon as he was awake. There was something filthy about them, Aya thought. Where they touched her, her skin burned and ached, and the act itself was dry and rough, sometimes painful. After they left, she would take cold showers and remain for long spells in the dark of her room to ease her discomfort, and shame.

She controlled her revulsion of men to be with David. She fought down her shame at being with a man, her fear of the filth he brought in with him, because there was a rare type of elegance about him, one akin to kindness, hope, healing. She had known another kindness, once, the one born of tenderness, in her mother's voice when she told her stories of long ago and her arms turned soft like velvet, and in her father's smile before the day took his smile away and wiped out the quiet joy of a family morning. A kindness that could not withstand the darkness that Kareem had dragged in.

When Aya first met David, she was struck by his demeanor. His gestures were slow and measured, his words, thoughtful and clear. Everything about him suggested a quiet, inoffensive, almost clinical detachment. There was no aggressiveness, no machismo. She let her guard down, and even her ingrained sadness temporarily subsided.

But now, for the first time, she sensed it, that masculine, unthinking violence, aimed straight at her. It was a violence bred in a certain understanding of love, a love that thrived on control, definition, imprisonment. That was what terrified her most, the claims of love on her, love that never lived up to its promises and that always ended in betrayal.

———

Aya's heart turned cold and a burning pain shot through her head. She rose unsteadily to her feet and felt his arm around her waist. She didn't want him touching her, but he didn't understand the sudden contraction of her body and he came closer, held her even tighter.

There was regret and embarrassment in his eyes. She sensed, more than she heard or felt, the anxiousness in his voice. He slipped a glass of cold water into her hand, a glass that smelled of dirt. Then suddenly, flashes of bright daylight, schoolgirls, prayers, a secret, a terror, a lonesome walk, a starry night and, above all else, the love song that came from her parents' bedroom in the cool of night.

David's love was an echo of these childhood recollections. Aya wanted to be back there, back in her parents' apartment, in the city she grew up in. She wanted to touch the purple bougainvilleas as they dropped, light and lush, around her window. She wanted to roll the ripe orange down her street and watch it bounce jaggedly down the brown cobblestones. She wanted to remember her glee at the pop and squish of dirty toes in blue-and-white plastic sandals. To hear the vibrations of the call to prayer on the whitewashed walls and cover her ears with her hands, running toward the nearest doorway and pressing her body against its hardness, beaten down by the unquenchable Mediterranean sun. Hearing always her parents' song that sang of love dying in the dance of time. The song that had always been *her* song.

Aya knew that David and she were doomed. She knew, just as surely as she knew that all the little gestures that once filled her days in Tangiers were slowly but surely becoming drops in the ocean of forgetfulness. It may be that all the loves in her life were doomed to fail, that her fate was solitude and aloneness with the voices in her head. Yet, she had learned to take comfort in the words whispered to her by the voices. Her fear was that her memory, too, would fail her. What would she do then?

When David asked that she move into his place, her head ached and the room began to spin. Why did he ask such things? Did he not understand she couldn't do what he asked? Did he not see?

The pain in her head half-blinded her and made her palms sweat. Her chest heaved and the air around her became scarce. It was all very wrong. David had pushed her to the breaking point. He meant to fill her with doubt, to hold her in his power. But why? She realized that she couldn't trust him, for she didn't know what his true intentions were.

It's strange, how the familiar can become distant, in the blink of an eye. David became a stranger to Aya as quickly as the tide ebbs.

Nothing about him was familiar to her anymore. His elegant build, his golden hair and strong hands, all belonged to a man with whom a tie had been severed in an instant. His eyes were no longer dark pools of violet, but neither were they kind and true. Who was this man standing in front of her, pacing like a caged bear? What was he hiding?

His pacing became more intense, his back the only part of him now consistently visible to her. He *was* hiding things from her. Had he figured it all out? Her secrets, her past hurt, her ultimate design and desire—had he known of them all along? Perhaps he had begun to suspect that she was on the brink of the greatest honor an artist could dream of and the blueblood in him couldn't accept that a mutt like her would become royalty.

These realizations burnt into Aya like hot rods meant to mark and enslave. She was unable to resist the waves of doubt and fear that rushed over her, spiraling out of control. When they finally subsided, an answer came to her, as clear as the images that danced and fought in her mind day and night.

He'd never loved her. And he knew about Ari. David knew that Ari wanted a painting of hers, that *her* work would be part of his great collection. And he couldn't stand it. He couldn't stand that she, too, would be anchored in history and posterity. His love was his way of keeping her bent, keeping her bound to him, tying her future to his. Aya had been different lately, intoxicated by her work. He knew she was on to something. David was in the business of being informed. Information was his key to the world, to power, to her. She was just another file to pursue diligently, to classify.

He knew about the quiet of her solitude, the well from which her work sprang, the brittle balance of her inner world. He was pushing Aya to her limits so that she could see the horrors at the edge.

David stared at her. He seemed to hesitate, to want to tell her something, but he just stood there.

The pain in her head was unbearable. She was losing control of her body and the room turned and turned around her like a merry-go-round unhinged.

He had never loved her, she saw now, she had never been his beloved. His kisses, his kindness had been ploys to seduce her into trusting him. And she had let her guard down.

Aya had crafted a self-image that insisted she was incapable of truly loving another person, because of the darkness inside her. Darkness that curled itself around her fingers when she brushed them against another's skin and put dampness where there should be warmth. That tugged at her when she yearned for forgetfulness in another's arms and turned the most inviting bed into a dreamlessness she could not rise from. That posed itself as her absolution from sins she'd never committed. It commandeered all the softness in her and condemned her to an aloneness she was never prepared for.

David's eyes, mouth, touch were all falsehoods honed to distract her from her purpose. The gentleness in his touch, the sunshine in his kiss, his golden hair and smooth skin all served to submit Aya to his will. He had opened her up, taken her into his world of effortless elegance to better ensnare her. With him, it was easy to forget who she was.

He had led her to believe that she could be repaired. But her roots were erased by her rise to success, and by David's society. She had tasted a fruit forbidden to people like her. His world, in fact, had been created to keep people like her out.

Aya never believed she was one of them. The more she tasted the glitter, the softness, the sparkle of this shining new world, the more difficult it became for her even to interact with other human beings. The heights were dizzying and the call of the void too strong for her to resist long. So she built walls and tricky subterranean passages and false roads that led nowhere, which she hid behind and that protected her from assaults.

Isolated, far from home, in a land that had given her everything, only the better to take it away. Aya, who had forgotten to cry for her homeland and for her mother and her father. She, who had believed that the scars of exile could heal. She, who thought talent and drive were enough to broker a peace. She, with the colorful scarf that had never touched her hair and the straight back that had never learned to bend, crumbling inside from an innocence that could not withstand the tests of time. She, who believed a canvas could save her.

seventeen

An answer arrived with the incoming twilight. Aya closed
her eyes and in it rushed, warm and cool, crystalline perfection—She must get rid of every human presence in her life.

Her thoughts spun like unfastened wheels. She needed
to push forward, in solitude, and devote her life to her work.
She couldn't allow herself any other purpose. Carnal dreams,
skin on skin, mouth against mouth, hair curled around fingertips, fantasies that embraced her thoughts as she stood,
brush in hand in front of the canvas, would all remain just
that—dreams, fantasies, cradles to her only purpose.

She would cease to exist, as a person, to the outside
world. She would forfeit gallery showings, phone inter-
views, written commentaries. Only then could she protect
herself, fulfill her promise, free of external hindrances and
distractions.

Everything grew calm and quiet. The desperation, the
urgency and fear that had gripped her for the past hours,
dissolved without a trace, except for a vague sensation of cold
and bitterness..

She opened her eyes.

She had forgotten Kareem. She must see him first. She
had to find out what he wanted, why he was there, if he *was*

Kareem—if he was even real. She cringed at her sudden doubt.

Her eyes adjusted to the surroundings and she was surprised by what she saw. There were torn books on the floor, shattered pieces of glass by the fireplace, a tray, a golden liquid seeping into the hardwood floor, broken chairs. David had his back turned, his arms rested on the marble mantelpiece and his head was lowered. He was completely still.

"David?"

He turned. His eyes were red. Why were his eyes red? He approached her, and embraced her tightly in his arms.

"Let me help you."

Aya looked at him, stunned, confused, angry. A little ashamed.

"Why would I need your help?"

"Do you understand what just happened here? Do you remember anything?"

She held her head high and lied, for all she remembered was a grief that should have died in the streets of Tangiers.

"Yes, I know what happened. Now I'd like you to leave. I'm tired."

His gaze on her was difficult to understand. He had become unknowable to her, a strange land adrift from her. Fear of Aya? No...fear *for* Aya. Why? She didn't have time to find out.

He came toward her, but she pushed him away.

His eyes deepened into dark pools of wild fire. Aya couldn't read him, but neither could he read her. His estrangement was her own. But this mustn't divert her. He was a danger to her, and to her purpose.

David stepped back, breaking the thin thread that still tied them together. Though he had soothed her suffering and offered her comfort, she realized, too late, that they had never been able to bridge the distance that separated them. He remained elusive, unknowable. He was her intimate stranger, her masked enemy. Who was he?

He walked quickly past her, picked up his dark, heavy winter coat and left. His scent, clean and deep, lingered in the room. His footsteps resounded on the wooden floors, the front door opened and shut, and then only the silence remained.

The sun came up, and dawn was suddenly upon her. Time had fled. She hadn't slept or gotten any rest. The strenuousness of the past hours weighed on her. The blue-pink sky was studded with the blinking city lights below.

She was alone. David was gone and she knew he would never come back. Her chest ached, her heart burned with yesterday's ill-consumed ashes.

She had to say goodbye to the past and to its lulling memories. To imagine a future as an American, safe from that Tangiers violence, tributary to another kind of violence that was foreign to her. But she didn't have the strength, or will, to step over the divide.

Aya needed to complete Ari's assignment. And David... Aya now had proof to back up her suspicions that he was her enemy, despite her doubt that he may not be so. David, with the glistening, light, carefree world he'd offered. A world that she had managed to scratch up, whose crooked secrets had opened up to her with such ease, like a red-blood flower blooming on an icy moor.

Aya watched the sun rise and listened to the buzz of traffic as it picked up speed and noise. Then she stood in front of the mantel mirror and looked at her reflection. The mirror was an antique, from the Art Deco era, her first purchase for her place in Cambridge. Art Deco mirrors were beloved in old Tangiers homes. Even for those families, like Aya's, who had fallen on hard times and could barely afford any luxury, an Art Deco mirror was the last luxurious possession to be abandoned.

The mirror was tall and oval, with bluish tints. It shimmered softly in the morning light like a large, tranquil pool of water. Aya rummaged through one of the drawers and took out a pair of scissors. She put the scissors down in front of the mirror, on the brick stones forming the mantel. She undid her hair and let it curl wildly around her neck. It was heavy and thick. It framed her face and swallowed her cheeks. It enlarged her yellow eyes and gave her skin a soft glow.

She took the scissors and cut off all her hair, watching the black-and-white curls fall on the wooden floor with barely a sound, around her feet. She stopped cutting only when her hair was cropped short around her ears, neck and forehead, looking like one of those young boys who claimed the Tangiers streets. She passed her hands through her hair. It was rough and soft. She shook out the remaining strands to the floor.

Aya felt cold. She wrapped her arms tightly around her chest. She felt her bones, the angles at which they stood out, the thinness of her frame, her frailty. Her body had weakened in the last few days. The weight had fallen off suddenly, and she hadn't even noticed. She gazed at her thin frame in the mirror. Her mouth opened wide and let out a soundless cry that became color in the blue-tinged mirror. Aya wanted to take back the screaming colors, though they were not her doing.

Her breath tainted its surface and the mirror became a hazy emanation of herself, as the colors blurred and the silhouette lengthened. She was terrified by what she saw in her reflection, the yearning and the sadness. She fought to retain control, for it was too early to let go, to slip into the peace that waited on the other side.

She straightened her back and adjusted her gaze. The colors and the silhouette gradually resumed their mundane places, and the bluishness of the mirror shined through once more.

Yet, it didn't matter, nothing did except the work that needed to be completed. For Ari would be coming to claim his due. She stepped across the glass doors into her studio and began working.

———

It was dawn, her preferred time of work, when the light accentuated the colors and shapes without unduly affecting or altering them. A time of day that created a perfect balance of sun and shade on canvas and opened it up, revealed the grayness beneath, to Aya, for her, like the first flower ever made, waiting for the hours to fill in its colors, to reveal its fullness, to unleash its hidden essence.

The painting had begun to reveal itself from within the folds of the canvas. It wavered on its surface. She could touch it. She knew what was expected.

She began to paint with a furious need that pulsated through her. She sweated it out and let it take control of her. It was a trancelike state that opened condemned doors in order to let the demons out. Painting became an exorcism of the pain, the loss and disillusionment that had woven themselves into her life and fought to take control of her.

The grays, browns and blacks, the splashes of purple and dots of blue, asked for brighter tints and hues. Colors spread like waves, streaming into the darker, heavier shades to light them up, to foil them, to break them. They signified nothing. Neither light nor night, neither joy nor despair. They stood for themselves.

Aya continued working throughout the day. The work pulled relentlessly at her, and every pause she took made her sick and anxious. She could not stop. She was like the refugee walking her road to freedom, which was also her exile, every step more painful than the next but every pause a brutal reminder of her loss and vulnerability. To walk was the only insurance she had that she would reach her destination.

Some claimed that painting was dead in the twenty-first century. They claimed that its flattened surface and contained space could not compete with the constant proximity of other mediums. Painting, they said, was about time and space, and the twenty-first century is about the implosion of time and space. She had thought so too in the beginning, but the repressed, the forgotten, have a tendency to return, tenaciously, viciously. And they said so many things. About her paintbrushes, about her canvases, her installations, about her. Yet, here she—and her brushes, canvases and installations—were. Together they'd survived oceans and changes. She had gone back to the paint, to the canvas.

Those who said that painting was a thing of the past, that the old art, queen of the arts, would soon die, had forgotten about those who cross oceans and leave their pasts behind them. They had forgotten about the likes of her and their desire for color, for painted life on a flat screen, for the golden hues of children's feet touching soft, brown sand beyond the roughness of white-and-gray seas.

With every brushstroke, Aya traced a new refuge. The painting was the ocean she needed to cross, at its edge a bit of light, of white, Tangiers, or perhaps, the lighthouse guiding her to the other side. Her legs were heavy, it was difficult to cross. Stones had been attached to her ankles, to sink easily and without a trace to the bottom of the sea. For they must have thought she would never make it. The gray waves rose and their white fangs cut through the humid air to drag her down to the waters' depths. The stones fell from her ankles and dropped into the water, paving their way through the mist and into the darkness below. She painted with fear and fury, in exhilaration, in hope.

The sun began to set. Its reddish hues, its golden oranges and soft purples, played on the canvas, adding to its own shades and lights, ageing it.

She put the brushes down and looked up at her work, gazing at what she had created, at what was beginning to take shape on the canvas, at its voluptuousness.

eighteen

You may wonder who she was, what kind of woman Mother must have been. You're tempted to call her a monster because you've forgotten the weight of family, of secrets and shame, as they are passed down the generations as quietly and as naturally as water that trickles downhill. You can't accept the weight of the past, unseen and unforeseen, on our membranes and on our lives, for you are turned toward what's ahead, toward the future.

———

She stood on the balcony, very still except for her dress that billowed in the wind, her tall, broad silhouette framed against the light. She heard footsteps behind her and turned, a smile brightening her tired face. The footsteps stopped, hesitant. She held out her hand, calling me to her.

It was not every day my mother was kind to me. I searched her face looking for signs of anxiety or anger or resentment. I had learned how to read those signs in the tightening of her jaws, the wrinkles that thinned beneath her eyes and the pinched, whitened nostrils. But her face was gentle, at peace. Today would be a light day, a day my mother would be my mother. A day that, perhaps, even you can picture, for it's not too unfamiliar.

I smiled back at her, and went to her.

"My Aya, my gentle Aya." She wrapped her arm around me.

We had a small balcony, more of a ledge than a proper balcony. But my mother had planted a small herb garden that hung out on the railings: mint, parsley, rosemary, basil and two small lemon and orange trees. She was proud of her modest garden. It was noticeable from the streets below, and conferred an air of grace and hope to an otherwise shabby, scratched façade. When she remembered to water it, like today.

There was barely enough space for the both of us on the balcony, but I was proud to be standing next to my mother, huddled against her large body, watching the bustle below and the seagulls above, flying toward the sea. Her voice cut through the silence and the peace. It lingers still as I write these words, for you.

"Do you know where your name comes from? Do you know why we called you 'Aya'?"

It wasn't a common name. It was short and slipped on the tongue, vowel after vowel. It wasn't a beautiful name, like Yasmine or Yacout, names of flowers given to beloved daughters. It wasn't an ancient, noble name, like Meryem or Alia. It wasn't a powerful name, like Fatimzahra or Khadija, the names of the prophet's daughter and beloved wife.

Aya. My name felt like a diminution, a breathlessness, a quickening of pace, an empty coffer.

"I waited a long time before having another child. Life was hard and it didn't seem fair to bring another one into the world. They say a child comes with its own blessings and we hoped for, needed a sign that the future would let up on us. Then you came. When you were born, your father was away. He had lost his job and went to Tetouan, nearby, to look for one. He wasn't back before three full days. And you remained, nameless and quiet, in my arms. You barely cried, I remember. You were the sweetest baby. Then your father came, and he saw you."

"What shall we call her?" he asked.

"Aya," I said.

"Aya. It came to me at that moment, a name I had never considered before. But it came, and it felt natural and right. Aya, like a prayer, a verse in the Qur'an. A sign, a miracle, a command. Our miracle, our answered prayer, our guiding command. That was what you were for me, for your father and I. We had placed our hope, our lives, in you, in the gift of your birth. A child comes to this world with her own blessings, they say. And Aya completed Dane well. Aya Dane. Your father said your full name, the sheep was sacrificed for you and Aya Dane was born. Only when your name was spoken and sanctified did you let out your first real cry. It was as though you took in your name, became alive through it, breathed it in. My Aya Dane."

I kept quiet. My mother's story had circled back upon itself to bite its own tail. It had come back and felt like a tight ring, a noose around me. She had bound me to her through that story, she had roped me in. I was Aya Dane, a prayer never answered, never fulfilled. A testament to their broken dreams, to their curdled expectations.

My mother had her own peculiar way of talking and pronouncing words. And my name never sounded or felt the same when other people said it. It was, in a sense, hers for the keeping. A name I could never separate from her, my estranged mother.

She held me close to her, and the scents from her herb garden, pungent and complex, became unbearable. Can you see it, you who are reading these lines from beyond the divide?

And you, too, close your eyes, for perhaps you have seen how the past, long forgotten, anew and renewed, can also be remembered in other ways, in light of the present, and of expected times to come. You've seen how it springs up in the most unexpected places, when you least expect it. You see it, like I do, in the intimacy of my art, in its precarious balance, in its trembling shadows.

nineteen

When Aya woke up, snow had fallen all night, and a shimmering carpet now covered the yards and pavements of Cambridge. She went to the window and took in the gentle whiteness all around. Trees, yesterday green and brown, were now enveloped in soft snow. She could hear children laughing in the distance and dogs barking. Families had begun putting up their Christmas trees, and windows were being decked in red, green and gold decorations. Even the city lights seemed to shine more golden, twinkling above the delicate carpet of snow.

She sniffed at this joy, but she couldn't *taste* it. She knew it was there, but it passed right by her, adorning the yard, the trees, the house below her lair with its lively decorations. She could see it in the full shopping bags that parents brought home from the store, hear it in the honks of truck drivers, smell it in the fragrance of hot cinnamon buns rising into the cold air. She watched from her distant perch as her neighbors began to receive parcels from loved ones, and, from behind a curtain, she couldn't help but be drawn to their smiling faces. The air was abuzz with the coming joyfulness. The holiday spirit had risen, and Cambridge and its residents seemed to bask in its warmth. And Aya magnified this happiness she was not a part of. Like other outsiders, she imagined perfection and joy in the lives of others, imagined a wholesomeness and happiness that, more often than not, didn't exist.

She brushed the window lightly with her fingers, still moist and caked with paint. Time had fled. Forty days—Ari had said that she had forty days to complete her work for him. A month had passed since the day she had received his invitation. Only ten days were left before he'd come for her work.

Her phone lit up. She didn't need to look to know who the message was from.

"When can I see you?"

"In three days."

"Where?"

"Beyond Longfellow Bridge. Cambridge side. Three o'clock."

"Thank you, darling. I'll count the hours."

"When I say the meeting is done, you go."

"With absolute certainty."

"And then I never want to see you again."

"As you wish."

Aya was ready to see her brother Kareem. She had thought long and hard about when and where to meet. Outside on the front porch? In the living room with the glass doors of the studio closed and locked? On the stairs or in the downstairs foyer where she was not "officially" living? Upstairs, beyond the white doors, in her apartment, in her art studio?

The lower part of the house, the entire downstairs area, had always been out of bounds to her. Not as a requirement of the original owners, who didn't mind where she chose to live, but because she had closed herself off to that part of the house. She chose to stay on the upper floor.

The owners had made their house as homey as can be. Its walls were covered in light-blue and warm burgundy paint. The couches were large and comfortable, the kind you can sink into with your hot cup of cardamom cocoa. There were large vases everywhere, as the mistress of the house—a gifted computer programmer—was also an accomplished flower arranger who insisted on decking the place with beautiful bouquets. Sometimes, she found crumbs on the couches. She would peer at them and wonder where they had come from. Odd. A mystery she couldn't resolve.

There were bedrooms: children's bedrooms, parents' master bedroom and guest bedrooms. The children's bedrooms were bright and modern. Bookshelves lined the walls and the desks were cut out for Apple computers, iPads and other such gadgets. The master bedroom had yellow-and-white walls, heavy curtains and funky brick walls. The guest bedrooms were as comfortably furnished, and as nondescript as high-end hotel rooms.

The children's bedrooms were the ones Aya had the most trouble going into. She would just stand at their doorways and peer in, feeling the way a still-wild cat must feel when her new owner takes her inside for the first time: Was the world not always a jungle? thinks the cat. Were the children safe?

Aya sniffed the softness and the lightness of the rooms. It was a scent she had never encountered. It triggered no gentle, regretful nostalgia. It elicited nothing. The rooms were exactly what they wanted to be: rational, secure, well-equipped spaces for well-groomed children, instruments allowing them to fulfill their—or their parents'—dreams. They spoke of such normalcy and predictability they made her hair stand on end. Do simple childhoods exist, she wondered? Are there happy, protected childhoods left in the world?

As time had passed, instead of finding it easier to walk through, see and take care of this space, Aya had found that it got harder. It soon became unbearable. It clawed at her every time she passed through. She began to see it as a larger-than-life mirror, created for the sole purpose of torturing her.

She hired a caretaker to come once a week to keep the family's home neat and dust free, and to make sure no flowers decked the vases. And she learned to avert her eyes and pretend there was no home breathing and sighing beneath her own. No home below holding up her home above.

Her thoughts ran and echoed one another inside her head. She could not rein them in. The only certainty she had, in the midst of all the sound and the fury, was that Kareem could not come *inside* her house. The idea of having him inside her home paralyzed her. He might want to sit in the "downstairs home," to look into the children's rooms, to open their books. He might want to see the "upstairs home," her space, her studio. His scent would be everywhere, and he might even refuse to leave.

She couldn't have him come inside her house. She couldn't allow anyone into her house anymore. People were unpredictable, and they carried with them their secrets, dragged in their demands. They ate you up and turned you in.

Aya had no other choice but to venture outside for one final time. That was when the idea of Longfellow Bridge occurred to her.

The bridge was just two hundred yards from her house. She could take medication to help her through the ordeal. She could walk hidden in a long coat and scarf, keep her head lowered and avoid people. She would meet him at a neutral place full of people who would pass them by but never touch them, speak to them, question them. And she would break it up whenever she wanted to.

Aya was ready. What she didn't expect was the meekness in his words and the resignation in his voice. And Aya, who had craved kindness ever since David left her, whose mind reeled with the needed solitude, trembled at the tenderness in Kareem's voice.

She was vigilant of his manipulation and the dangers he could pose. His violence and cruelty were sugarcoated in words of love and care. Yet they were emptiness itself. Nothing in his words rang true. Lies had mingled with violence ever since that night when he returned to their parents' home, after his unexplained disappearance. But before that day, and all the days after that, there had been a time when his tenderness was truth itself.

An acute, violent pain turned everything dark.

twenty

Kareem and Aya lived with their parents in a once bus-tling quarter of old Tangiers. Neighbors would share meals through open doorways and satellite dishes across narrow streets and flat rooftops. Milk, honey and flour would descend and ascend in baskets through wires fixed between buildings and floors. Laughter and words also descended and ascended to fill the air with a buzz and a lilt. The bougain-villea fluttered in the breeze, and the warm smell of sweet, fried donuts rose from the street vendors. Ambition was kept in check, and those who dreamed of the world or of thicker wallets readily left, for this was not a place to dream of the world and its riches.

Sometimes beautiful stories were heard, and sometimes terrible stories came through. No one in the neighborhood recalled the precise moment when the terrible stories began to outnumber the beautiful ones.

It must have happened surreptitiously, stealthily, in the night, in the dark, when no one was watching. Tangiers had closed in upon itself, as one by one its young, denied a fu-ture, shriveled, like leaves in an autumn come too soon. New voices from the East filled in their empty days, and the call of the land beyond the short strip of sea became overpowering.

They stepped into the brightly colored wooden boats and were soon returned, lifeless, to the shore.

The sea—which none in this neighborhood could see from their apartments or their homes unless they climbed to the highest rooftops, looked out beyond the white-gray of the city and plunged their gaze into its blue—had begun to cast away bodies without distinguishing between male and female, adult and child, sanding down the skins and smoothing over the faces. The numbers swelled and grew, unnatural waves of unutterable sadness.

The sighs rang through the city and the neighborhood plunged into an icy, superstitious fear that stifled hope and joy. Many of the bodies returned by the sea were its own.

The neighbors buried their dead and the neighborhood streets now rang with cries ascending and descending, dark veils covering the windows where once bright ropes hung taut between buildings and women's light fingers pushed a basket from one windowsill to the next.

But beautiful stories, though rare, could still be heard. For many of the inhabitants, Kareem was one of these beautiful stories.

Kareem was cherished by parents, by friends and neighbors alike. He charmed his way out of trouble and dazzled with his quick smile and dark, mischievous eyes. He was carefree and easy. He brought lightness to a place that had learned to weave gloom into its future. He was lightning quick with his feet. A star football player, a ticket out. The next Zidane, our Ronaldo, his coaches and friends said as they slapped him on the back or held him in a bear hug. At fifteen, it was impossible to deny his talent. He played in difficult conditions and with little means: he played in the dirt fields on the outskirts of town or in the patched field sometimes lent to the school by the local administration. He played with new balls, old balls or soda cans. His feet danced.

A great deal of hope was placed in Kareem. By the time he reached his fourteenth birthday, his school coach thought it was time he competed in tryouts in one of the biggest junior clubs of Tangiers, the one that was funded by the most prestigious Spanish football clubs and allowed the best young players to find a place in Spanish football.

Kareem was ready. He was excited and tense. His parents had never seen him wired so tightly and sweating so profusely. Aya was the only one to notice that he acted a little strange, not the usual, cheerful brother she knew, but she pinned it on the stress of the tryouts.

The day of the tryouts, his coach came to pick up Kareem and his father. His mother and the neighborhood women worked in the kitchen to prepare sweet almond snacks, honeyed Moroccan pancakes and pomegranate juice, for they were ripe and thick at this season. They heated the water and poured it into the traditional teapot. They added chunks of sugar and grains of black tea. Finally, they cut fresh, wet mint leaves and pushed them delicately into a curved teapot. They took out a large silver tray that her mother displayed only for the most festive times, and set the pot upon it. They surrounded the curved teapot with twelve thin, delicate tea glasses.

Then the women sat, in a tight-knit circle in the narrow living room, on the brown sofa accented with yellow lace. Decked in their finest embroideries, makeup and dresses, they chatted and laughed like women do when men are absent. They were waiting for Kareem, ready to sound their high trills and stomp their feet, like women are known to do in northern Morocco, where the sounds of Flamenco and

Sevillana accompany the child in her white laced crib, the bride in her nuptial bed and the old woman on her deathbed. For Kareem to be selected to the Spanish-sponsored football club, despite petty jealousies and brief pangs of envy, would be a triumph, a moment of pride for the entire neighborhood. Their neighborhood, often mentioned in the newspapers for its numerous deaths at sea, its drug busts and fanatic Islamism, would now be praised for the talents of one of its sons.

And so the women sat, fluffing up their fineries, ready to embrace the mother and hold her in their arms, she, the mother of all mothers and he, Kareem, the son of all sons. When the door finally opened, it was late in the afternoon; the sun had disappeared behind the pink minarets and the women were ill at ease.

The father came in first, followed by the coach and finally Kareem. One look at her husband's face and the mother knew that things had gone wrong. The other women, used to things going wrong, for that was the way of their world, rose to their feet, picked up their scant belongings and scurried out the door. For the one or two curious women who tried to lag behind, a harsh word, a slap on the backside or the head by the other women, and there they were, hurrying as fast as they could out the door.

The parents remained in the living room with the coach and Kareem. They spoke in soft voices, and Aya strained to hear what they were saying, but still she could not. She heard her father's worried tone and her mother's tears; she heard the anger and disgust in the coach's voice and the deafening, heartbreaking silence of Kareem.

She understood that her brother would not be going to Spain, to star-studded Madrid, to train on real football fields.

She also understood, beyond this immense disappointment, that something else had happened. Something even more terrible and unspeakable.

What soothed her was that Kareem did not seem to mind his failure. Nothing in his behavior hinted at any disappointment or frustration.

No one could have said, encountering Kareem as he walked down a street or turned a corner: "Ah. Here's a young man who knows what it's like to have his dream shattered. You can see it in the darkened corner of the eye, in the tired step, in the stooped back and gray fingernails." Physically, Kareem remained the same.

It was his interests, however, that shifted. He did not play ball anymore, and his teachers complained, when they noticed, that he often missed school. He tore down the football posters from the bedroom wall and let his sneakers sit on the windowsill, taking in the wind, rain and humidity of a bitter winter.

Aya did not care whether Kareem became a football star. Nor did she care if he made it or not in some fancy football club she had never heard of in her life.

He was her hero. Her adoration of him was that of a little sister for an older brother but also that of a little girl protected and spoiled by a doting sibling. She could not imagine life without him. When she got out of school, she would run home, hoping to find him there, the door to the room always open for her, just for her.

He had many girlfriends and went through them as quickly as he burned through a cigarette. He liked to say to her, "You and Mother are the loves of my life," and Aya would feel her heart melt and her cheeks blush in happiness. Kareem laughed easily, and his warmth was contagious.

She cherished her brother's words and never repeated them to a soul. They were the secret that always made her feel special, even when she met the sophisticated girls at her brother's arm and realized she would never look like them. They laughed, at ease, confident in their youthful beauty, their curled hair, bright lipstick and carefully applied black eyeliner, their cheeks blushing when he bent toward them to kiss them, and their teeth white and pointy when they smiled up at him. Aya knew they would come and go, and that she would stay.

Her mother would shrug her shoulders and say, "Boys will be boys," but her father remained silent. He only spoke up once, when he heard a girl crying in the street below, as Kareem came up the stairs, whistling a popular tune, oblivious, it seemed, to her pain. The father said to the mother, "I never loved anyone but you. I never wooed anyone but you. I don't think I ever made a girl cry—and I certainly didn't whistle, as I left her."

The mother told him to lighten up and not put cruel intent where there was only fun and games. Times had changed and these girls knew what the risks were. Her eyes burned with love for her son, they flashed with pride in him. The father remained quiet, though he thought of how one was never too young to be kind, nor too old to be cruel.

Aya did not see Kareem the way her father and mother saw Kareem. He was the person she felt closest to and the one she looked up to. When he came to pick her up at her school, she knew the rest of the day would be perfect. When he ruffled her hair and told her she was the only one in his life, she felt her heart would burst. Aya believed he could do no wrong.

One day, Aya heard a girl crying. The sobs came from the room Aya shared with Kareem. Soon after, the door opened and footsteps rang in the hallway. She had been studying problem sets in her father's office. She put down her pencil and paused. She was not mistaken, someone was sobbing outside Kareem's door. She opened the door, carefully.

A girl was crying in the hallway. Her black eyeliner was streaming down her cheeks, and she was trembling like a leaf blown this way and that by the wind. Her lips were full and her eyes a deep gray. Her beauty was undeniable, despite her distraught appearance. She stopped when she saw Aya. She touched her cheek with her delicate, trembling hand.

"You're the little sister, aren't you?"

Aya looked at the girl, not much older than she, and saw the pain and fear in her eyes. Aya stood very still, feeling the cool of the girl's hand on her cheek flowing through her body.

"You seem like a sweet little kid. Don't be fooled by him. He's not what you think he is."

Aya looked at her, confusion and anger brimming her eyes. She stepped back and went running into her father's office.

"Doesn't anyone here understand? Don't any of you see what he is?"

Aya could still hear the girl crying. Then she heard her heels clicking on the hallway's mosaic floor and the front door closing behind her.

Kareem knocked softly on the office door. When he opened it, he found her sitting at the desk, reading a book, or pretending to. He ruffled her hair and bent toward her:

"What are you reading, my darling?"

Aya closed the book. Kareem picked it up and flipped through the pages.

"You know St. Exupéry crashed his plane in our desert?"

She nodded.

"Many European explorers and adventurers have disappeared in our deserts..."

She didn't answer and kept her head stubbornly down.

"Ah…I see you met Lila. She's a nice girl, but she can't stay forever, can she, darling?"

Aya looked up at him, eager for an explanation. But none followed. Kareem said.

"…You're doing well in school?"

"Yes."

"I hear you came in first in the national mathematics exam?"

Aya smiled.

"Yes."

Kareem frowned.

"I hope you didn't smile that way at the examiner. Was he a man?"

She blushed.

"You see. Women and math, the Imams say that's not possible. Women's brains are not wired that way. And yet here you are…and isn't that strange? Unless, you're hiding something from me?"

There was an indescribable tone in his voice. She struggled to make sense of it, to understand where this new harshness, this mockery, this sarcasm came from. She felt the tears streaming down her face. Huge, unstoppable tears. She could feel him standing behind her. He held her head in both his hands, squeezing tight, as though trying to empty it of its content. Then, he laughed. A low, bitter laugh that chilled her to the bone. And he walked out.

Aya stayed at the desk, her back straight, her hands clenched into fists, as the tears fell. She felt alone in the world, her thoughts whirling around in her head like an abandoned child on a merry-go-round.

Later that night, the mother and father came into their

room. They sat on the bed and called her name. To the outsider looking in, here was a family scene like there are all
over the world. The room was small and warm. The parents
sat on the bed and spoke to their daughter, as parents do and
as parents should. Yet, if that outsider had only peered in a
little closer, if she had looked at the child's face and hands, at
the father's feet and the mother's brow, she would have seen
that the scene was not what it seemed, and she would have
let them be, for it was too late for them.

The mother spoke first.

"Your brother, don't listen to what strangers say of him
or what he himself says to you. This is a complicated period
for him."

"He got kicked off his team. He cheated at the tryouts.
The most prestigious tryouts in the country! He ruined his
chance at a better life. He brought that upon himself. He has
only himself to blame for his wrongdoing," the father said.

The mother sucked in her breath and defended her son.

"Kareem was always the best player, his coaches loved
him."

"You know what he did. He deserved his punishment."

"Was he punished because he did wrong, because he
used something they all use and *he* got caught, or because
the other parents had connections that we did not?"

"What does it matter? His punishment was fair, his
release was not. He took something. Isn't that enough? He
should learn from his mistakes."

"You use your logic and outdated ethics for a country
that only knows brute force and lies. They all lie, they all
cheat, and they all get ahead. And he, our precious boy, will
be sacrificed because you refused to pay the amount they
asked for."

"Let them lie and cheat. My son is not like them. And I will never pay to cover up for him."

"He didn't stand a chance against those other kids."

"He was good enough. He would have made it."

"And now we'll never know."

"It's not too late. He can try again next year."

"What choice did he have? What are his options now?"

"The very thoughts that should have crossed his mind."

"That's the way it works. This is *his* reality. You've forgotten what it feels like to dream."

"You're right, I don't remember the hope. I remember the disappointment that follows."

"Who can stop a young man from dreaming? Who is to blame?"

"Yes, who is to blame…"

Her father lowered his head, and Aya looked at her parents, at her father's defeat and her mother's pain. She didn't know what they were talking about. She only understood that Kareem would no longer be going to school and that he might, or might not, be responsible for it. Finally, Aya didn't see how this related to her or to the sad, delicate girl she had seen in the hallway. She waited.

"Aya," her father said, "your mother and I can't agree about *him*, and I don't think we ever will. Mothers and their sons, they create their own world and they allow no one in. I say this to you, my daughter: Never doubt yourself, never sell yourself short and find a way to leave this place. If it means to forget all this, us, your mother and me, your roots and your history, then so be it."

Her father's words drifted into the air. Aya wished she could grasp them, hold them, gather them to her and harness their strength. But they were just words, slight and wispy like ghosts, weak and immaterial; the forsaken promises of deserted lands.

She had trouble breathing and while her head still hurt where Kareem had pressed it, she was slowly regaining control of herself. She now felt detached. Her parents had left the room and she remained alone. Her eyes widened and her knuckles turned white. She was only now fully realizing how alone she had always been.

twenty-one

A few days earlier, when Aya came home from school, she heard a sound like music or incantations coming from their room. For those of his family members who wished to see, as the door, for once, was wide open, Kareem was sitting on his bed, a rolled, half-smoked cigarette next to him on the desk as he held the Holy Qur'an upside down in his hands. The Qur'an was blasting from his computer: a long-bearded, grim-faced, self-proclaimed Imam hitting the faithful with his rough, harsh reading of the Book.

If only they had wished to see and had bothered to enter his room, they would have then seen Kareem holding the cigarette joint between his left index finger and his middle finger and burning the skin on his forearms with it. They would have seen older and deeper scars and burns crisscrossing his forearms, his thighs and his torso.

The ashes that had mingled with the singed skin fell on the open pages of the Book. Kareem did a peculiar thing. He let the reddish-gray ashes slip into the binding between the pages. Then he slammed the Book shut and opened it again. The ashes marked and seared the pages.

If they had come even closer to him, they would have seen the hollow despair in his eyes.

And if they had listened carefully, their heads close to his, perhaps they would have heard him whisper to himself, as he burned his forearms with the cigarette. "Death, death, death."

If the parents had stepped through his wide-open door into the bedroom.

But they didn't.

twenty-two

A week had passed. Aya hadn't left her studio or turned on the TV since David had walked out her door. Her relief was profound. It was easy to imitate the clutter of life despite the lack of human presence.

Her only human contact was the music that filled the studio. Bach, his Goldberg Variations, with Glenn Gould humming like mad in the background. Her work had deepened, and the paint she applied had thickened to form a texture between oil and solid matter. She could almost grasp it, converse with it. She saw in it shadows of herself and saw herself as the pale reflection of the passion she had poured into its composition.

Three days had passed and she needed to gather the strength to meet Kareem at the Bridge. She pushed the canvas into a corner and turned off the lights in the studio. She stepped through the glass doors into the living area and noticed the paint on her hands and arms.

For once, the fusing, messy colors on her arms and hands bothered her. She usually enjoyed the way the paints took over her skin—cocky, temporal tattoos whose claim over her she wore with pride. She usually liked how they marked her, toyed with the light brown of her skin, slipped under her nails and enhanced the lines of her palms. But, for once, they appeared dirty and toxic to her. The colors were tentacles crawling up her hands and arms, penetrating her pores, suffocating her skin.

She went into the bathroom, took a long shower and scrubbed her body red. The colors fell, liquid and pale, off her skin and down the drain. With a thick towel, she dried off the specks that remained.

She stood in front of the mirror, naked and raw like a newborn child. She touched her head, letting her fingers run down her scalp and across her neck. Only her eyes showed her fear, her hollowness, her exhaustion. Her age. She realized that suddenly, in her thirties, at the height of her talent and beauty, she was old. It was not about age or firmness of breast or strength of limb; it was about what was going on in her mind. And her mind was that of an old woman who had crossed many seas and left many lands behind her.

It was the mind of one who has said goodbye, long ago, to everything she held dear, knowing she would never return. The mind of one who has lost a child, a family, a home, a warmth, a tenderness, a dream, a sleep. It was the mind of one who was abandoned by nostalgia itself, whose memories played her and played with her, imprisoned her and only revealed themselves to confuse and entrap her.

The mind of an exile, one whose mind was exile itself.

She opened the cabinet behind the mirror and took out a bottle of pills. She swallowed the ones she needed to be able to leave her house and confront Kareem at Longfellow Bridge. The buzz, she knew, would soon hit her with its comforting lull.

She wore her usual black outfit and large, colorful scarf. She outlined her lips in nude and her eyes in black. She gathered her coat and handbag, and went down the stairs through the main living room. She crossed it and reached the front door. Trembling, she touched the doorknob and turned it.

That was when she heard a sound, music both familiar and unfamiliar, at once most intimate and distant. It was the sound of a guitar playing in the street. The guitar was playing Christmas carols, but the way each phrase ended was peculiar. Their ending reminded her of the Sahara Desert, of nomads crossing the sands on a night filled with stars, of old West African tunes.

She turned her back to the front door and went to the window. She pushed aside the heavy beige curtains and saw the musician. He was a tall, thin black man and he held the guitar in his arms like a mother holds her newborn child. He sang to the tune and his voice was as pure and beautiful as the sound of a stone falling into a well of deep, clear water.

He raised his eyes and he too saw Aya. He smiled and his smile made her forget the cold and the loneliness of a Cambridge winter. She opened the window a crack.

He came toward her and stopped right below the window. "Salaam, *ma soeur*."

Aya hesitated.

"Aalaikoum assaloum, *mon frère*."

"Where are you headed, on this cold, frightful day?"

"To meet my brother. He's waiting for me."

"Is he now, *ma soeur*?"

She was quiet. She found herself smiling at this stranger, filled with a peace she hadn't felt in a long time. She thought how cold he must be, with the snow falling all around him and his arms wrapped around his guitar. She leaned against the windowsill. She could, after all, stay with him just a little bit longer.

"And what is your name, little sister?"

"Aya Dane. *Et toi, mon frère?*"

"Ali Falo Taré, of Timbuktu in Mali."

She was curious.

"And, how did you, Ali Falo Taré of Timbuktu in Mali, find yourself here, in the streets of Cambridge, playing classical Christmas tunes on a guitar such as yours?"

The tall man smiled back and told her he was a renowned guitar player back home, one of the most celebrated musicians in Mali. He was part Songhai and part Fula. "The Malian Blues," he howled, "that's my thing, little sister. In the tradition of Ali Farka Touré, greatest musician of all, Grammy Award winner, if you please."

Aya's smile broadened. He was not a modest man. But his music did not lie.

He had left Mali after the destruction of Timbuktu, in 2010. A refugee, pure and simple. "But I have family here, in Boston," he explained, all the while strumming his magical guitar and bringing tears of loss to her eyes. "My sister, she married an American. Ah, yes, she is one happy girl, not like you. You carry the world on your shoulders, *ma soeur.*" And he raised his hands up at her, his eyes twinkling and amused.

"Why so sad? You have made it to America, you should be thankful. You have papers, no doubt. You should be oh so thankful! Bless that God that you don't believe in, fool, *folle.* He brought you here. And why are you standing up there, your face half-hidden by those ugly white-people curtains? Come down here, or invite me up, like a true *Africaine!* Give me some of that world-famous tea of yours."

"I can't go down to you. I'm sick. I can't invite me up. I'm in a hurry, you see."

"Ahhh…the sickness of the city, that's what got you. You have the homesickness, *ma soeur*. Sometimes it gets to people and it never leaves them. It's a curse."

"No," Aya shook her head. "Not homesickness, brother. I'm adrift."

"So, *qu'est-ce qui ne va pas, petite soeur?* Tell your brother, your musician straining to hear the words from your mouth."

"What eats at me is the feeling that I will never be safe again."

"And who's ever safe? It's an illusion."

"And the illusion is what counts, *grand frère*."

He strummed his guitar and sang a song.

"For you. I will remember you when I am up there and you are still in your home. Trembling with fear, doing *shit* with your life."

"Don't you know, brother? I stay here, I don't leave my house. But I am known. A famous artist."

His laugh resonated and the sidewalk shook.

"You? *Ma soeur*, I am now most worried about your health."

"Look me up. I do not lie. Aya Dane."

"The name is familiar…I too am going to be famous someday, again. I will start all over again. Bigger. Isn't that the American Dream?"

"The American Dream?"

"I embrace it, unlike you. I believe we, West Africans, our destiny is here, in this land. The blood shed here by our forefathers, the enslavement, the history, it is all for *us*. Our destiny is America."

He held out his long, strong hands and Aya gave him hers. His hands were warm while hers were cold. He heated them like fire between his. It was her turn to laugh.

"*Quand tu seras grand, mon frère,* when you will be great, play the blues for me on that guitar."

"That I will."

He turned and Aya watched his tall, lean frame recede in the whiteness of the street.

She believed him now. She believed he was a master musician in Timbuktu, and she believed that, somehow, he would succeed in his chosen land. And that belief uncoiled her heart and conquered her fear, even if only for a little while.

When Ali Falo Taré's frame had disappeared around the corner, Aya closed the window and pulled back the curtain on the street. She turned away from the window, crossed the living room and went up the stairs, back to her lair.

twenty-three

Aya paused at the door. She was forgetting something important. She couldn't return to the studio's peace and quiet just yet.
Something *big*, something *dreadful* was supposed to happen
today. She was supposed to meet someone. Someone important, who had asked to see her and whom she had agreed to see.
Someone who had meant a great deal to her in the past.

She struggled to remember who that person was, or why
she had to meet him. Her head felt heavy and her body weak.
Through the tall glass doors, she crossed into her studio. The
room spun wildly while she tried to regain her balance. Just
before she closed the doors behind her, she remembered
whom she needed to see, who was waiting for her beyond
her front door, on the other side of the yard. Her brother,
Kareem.

She couldn't rest just yet, She couldn't fold the world behind her, because Kareem was waiting for her. She left the studio and went down the thin white stairs into the foyer below.
She stepped across the threshold and locked the front door.

———

She walked hurriedly toward the bridge, the first stars shining
above and the Charles River glistening ahead. At first, she

didn't see him. She thought, for a hopeful split second, that he had chosen not to come, that it had all been a bad dream.

It was then that she saw a thin, gaunt figure, dressed in black, a hood covering his face, hiding his features from view. Though she hadn't seen him in fifteen years, and her brother had been an athletic, broad-shouldered young man in his youth, she knew it was him. The way he swayed slightly, the way he stared into the black waters…

He was looking out toward the river, his hands deep inside his pockets against the bitter cold.

She called out, "Kareem."

She had startled him, and it pleased her. He turned to her and his face was as gaunt and thin as the rest of him. Aya stared into his eyes, and he realized, before she did, that he still terrified her.

But the fear didn't taste the same, it didn't fill her mouth the same way. It didn't hold her in its claws with the same ease as in the past. Whereas once she feared his physical presence, his strange, warm breath on her neck, his cold, sweaty hands on her back, that brutal fear was now gone, replaced by the shock of seeing him so diminished. What she feared now was the memories his presence called up and the monsters he could unleash.

His eyes thinned to a line and his smile stretched across his face like a scream. His presence, forlorn and out of place, echoed her emptiness.

"Fifteen years. A lifetime, gone in a whiff."

He looked around, clumsily flailing his arms, like a windmill broken by the sudden fury of the wind.

"What is this place? Why are you here?"

She didn't answer. It was safer not to, she instinctively knew, for old stories never die and she was already tuning in to his cruelty as though no time had lapsed. Instead, she repeated his question to him and smelled the violence that lurked beneath his stooped shoulders and thin arms.

"Why are you here, brother?"

He wasn't smiling anymore. He passed his hands over his graying hair, and she could see the veins that lined his hands and forearms. She then saw that his thinness was ironclad and that she had underestimated his strength. He inched closer.

"Look around, little sister. The waters are dark, the people hard like snow. And these buildings... they look like prisons."

Night was falling and the few people still out were huddled under their winter coats, their breaths cold wisps in the icy air. And because she didn't answer him, he answered her:

"I came because I was finally free to come. They let me go. And now I'm here, and I came to get you. To take you home. We could be a family again."

"Who let you go? Where were you?"

Kareem breathed heavily.

"It's not important. What matters is that I'm here now. And that I want you to return home with me. You belong with me. You always have."

She stood still. The quiet of the night had taken over. Her childhood terrors had returned with a vengeance, as though they had never left, but had merely turned their backs on her and now had turned to face her again. He understood this. He had always seen through her, known how and where to press, where it hurt the most.

She took a deep breath, remembered she was safe now, that she could no longer be defined by what was taken from her.

"No. I belong here. Tangiers is my past, and so are you."

His laugh rang out, shrill and hollow.

"This place? This country, it will swallow the world. And you with it, a tiny speck of nothing in their greater ambition. If you come with me, I'll make it all up to you. We'll build a real life, a meaningful life, from scratch, you and I."

She slipped from his embrace, the way she used to as a little girl.

"Where are our parents?"

"No one told you? Or perhaps you don't remember? They did say there was something wrong with you, but I couldn't believe it."

She sunk her heels into the ground, straightened her back. "I know that you are someone who destroys things... homes, families, trust. That's what I know."

"You want to know what happened, don't you? You want to know why they sent you away?"

"They didn't send me away. It was for the best. It was because of you."

"Because of me?"

The shrill laugh rang out once again in the deserted city air, rippling through the frozen waters and the stone bridge. Kareem now grabbed her shoulders, close to her neck. She sensed his strength, beneath his thin, gray arms. And she saw that his hands and the small of his wrists were perhaps not as pale and weak as she thought. There was a tinge of gold, of reddish-brown, of unbreakable purpose. A piece of the old country still blazed through him. He was warming up against her, to her, despite her, like embers to air.

"There was...a fire," she remembered. "It burned everything. But that was after I left. Yes, that's right. It was... You..."

Kareem interrupted her.

"The question is, why did they send you away?"

For the first time, there was discomfort, even fear, in his attitude.

"Because *he* came, to save me."

"They sent you away because you were a burden. A shame. Because they didn't know what to do with you anymore. You were our shame. You had given it away, and there was nothing left inside you."

It was all a trick. He used words as fabrications to mystify and mislead. He was here to break what was still whole, to empty out the dregs. His voice interrupted Aya's reflections.

"Come back with me, all will be better. I will even show you where our parents are. You will understand. You will find the answers you're looking for."

To go back. A sunken desire as hard and pure as a diamond, but one that Aya could not submit to.

She understood then that this meeting, after fifteen years of silence, would resolve nothing. She understood that Kareem was not here to admit, apologize, or concede, but instead to defeat once more, to bend, to take. He was of the race of takers, of those who burst open the fruit and smell out its budding tenderness. And she must not give in to him, no matter how many voices screamed inside her head or how great the pain behind her eyes.

"There is no trust left between us. Those ties have brought only betrayal and cruelty. I will not go with you. If I choose to return, it will be in my own way."

"What am I supposed to do now?"

"Go back. Go back before they see you for who you are and break you down."

"Break me? It's too late for that. There's nothing they can do to me now. Don't you see yet?"

Kareem stood in front of her, haggard and gaunt. Still, Aya didn't relent. She knew too well the games he played, the manipulation, the perversion. Time stood still and all was quiet. They let it take over, surround them. Finally, Kareem's voice cut through the silence.

"When you and I were children, we would go down to the beach. On the way, we'd stop because you'd want a treat—honey-sweet almonds, grilled sunflower seeds, loose nougat. I always had a couple of coins in my pocket, for you. It was often just the two of us; Mother had her headaches, and Father, his work, and I would take care of you." His voice trailed off.

Kareem must have understood then that she would never believe him again, that she would never again bend, that his syrupy persuasion would never work on her again.

His shoulders slumped forward, his foot drew a circle in the snow and his fingers tugged at his pants. His attitude suddenly changed from sly confrontation to shy regret. And in this new stance, which could only be a ruse, was a new demand, a plea for her compassion, for forgiveness.

There was surrender, unexpected and haunting, in his voice.

"Childhood is what can't be written down."

She couldn't look into his eyes. It wasn't because she feared him still. It was because she felt nothing. And this hardness of the soul, this absolute rigidity, came to her unexpectedly, as though it had always lain in wait, beyond her control or knowledge.

"You lie. All you do is lie, deceive, cover up. I'm done with you."

Aya turned to walk away. A moment later, a shot rang out and the air was filled with the sound of a body falling to the ground.

She didn't need to turn around to know what had happened. She thought of the brown body on the white snow, and the red that spread from the heart, like a broken porcelain rose. She closed her eyes and knew that her brother lay on the ground, and that it was finally over. The wall inside her cracked and revealed the shame it had kept in. All the barriers broke, one by one, leaving her facing an emptiness. And inside that emptiness was a raging sea, stone-cold waves and chalk-white foam that transformed into letters, after which letters transformed into words, words into sentences, and sentences into a vast scroll that grated at the water's surface.

She exhaled.

"Kareem."

And walked on.

She thought about the softness that had appeared in his eyes, in his hand tugging at his pants, in his final words. She wondered what would have happened if she had let the softness in and bent to his demands. But she hadn't, and the air tasted sweeter and the flowers on her scarf bloomed and waved gently in the cool, sparkling twilight.

She had reached her attic when a terrible pain seared through her.

twenty-four

Their mother found Kareem and Aya in the room they shared. Aya was bleeding from the middle, slightly, just a drop on the lower end of her pajama top. She was holding an old doll in her right hand. Kareem was sitting at his desk, his fingers strumming a tune on the front cover of the Qur'an.

When the mother walked in, he handed her a bottle of water and pointed at Aya. "Give her a drink and get her out of here," he said.

"What happened here, my children? What happened?"

Kareem shrugged his shoulders and left the room. Aya was now alone with the mother. Her body hurt all over, but she couldn't quite pinpoint the source of the pain, yet. Her mother stared at her pajamas and covered her with a blanket. She avoided looking at the single red drop of blood on Aya's pajama pants, near her lower abdomen.

She found she couldn't tell the mother the truth. She couldn't blame her brother and say, "He did it. My brother did it." For, in truth, she wasn't even sure what he had done. She knew it was a shameful thing, and yet she sensed that he felt no shame. It was hers alone.

She wanted to talk to her mother and tell her what had happened, but the memories of the event were quickly fading. She tried to hold on to them, but they were blurry and slippery. It was like a nightmare from the day before: come the next night, the nightmare is already half-forgotten, though the dread of the dark is there to stay. The truth, the facts, were nowhere to be found, for they had found nowhere to remain.

Aya looked into her mother's eyes and sensed that she, too, didn't want the truth. Her mother nodded and held out her hand to Aya. Her eyes were dry. She never brought up the incident again. She never spoke about it to anyone. She never looked at Aya the same way again. She never confronted her son or confided in her husband, parents, or friends. She never played her Leonard Cohen love song again. And she never smiled again.

The only tenderness she would now show her daughter was at night, when Aya couldn't sleep. She would sit by her bedside with a glass of tea in her hands and tell her stories to ward off the darkness hovering nearby. And when Aya awoke the next morning, she would see the blackened tea grains at the bottom of the delicate glass and she would remember.

The only tenderness she would now show her son was when he woke up in the morning and she heated up his breakfast, before the streets ate him up for the day.

Though she never mentioned the incident to anyone and gave no sign that this was connected to the little red drop of blood on her daughter's pajamas, she cleared her husband's office, a narrow room at the far end of the hallway, and moved Aya in. "There, dearest, your own room. You're growing up so fast." She threw her doll in the garbage can. "You won't be needing this anymore, Aya. No more silly children's games."

And Aya, her eyes lowered, waited for the mother to leave. Then she picked up the doll from the garbage can and hid her beneath her pillow. "There," she said softly, "you can hide there for a while."

As their mother now was only a mother to her children at bedtime and at breakfast time, and their father seemed unaware of what was happening under his own roof, Kareem's power grew.

He started telling Aya to wear the veil, the black veil, to cover her filth. He did not think a simple veil was enough. He demanded the entire burqa, the black cloth that would cover a woman completely from head to toe.

He wants me dead, Aya thought. *He wants me as absence to my presence. Covered in black from head to toe, denied contact with the sun and air and moon. The world denied contact of me, remembrance of me. He wants the world to think of me as darkness and he wants me to think of the world as darkness. He wants me dead and he wants the world to see me and remember me only as the Dead One. I will not.* Aya touched the red, burning spot he had left between her legs. *I will not.* And something inside her shattered for good.

The father and the mother put up a pale resistance to him. But Kareem never forced himself on her again. Perhaps, since he had taken from her what his kind considered most sacred, he had no need left for her. Perhaps he was busy elsewhere. Or perhaps he feared the new protection Aya's accomplishments in school had brought her. A protection in the shape of a man.

A man. Tall, quiet and foreign. People said he was the son of an American, a passing traveler, an *expat*, but that his mother was Arab, of Jewish faith. She had him with this passing traveler, a man who had said and promised he would stay, but who left with the dawn. They said she was madly in love with him, that she sewed lace pillows and bed covers, in the way of her Spanish ancestors, that told of their love and her past, for them to contemplate before lying with each other. They even said that she had started to make a white lace *mantilla* for her wedding day. She also took out the mother-of-pearl *peineta* that her grandmother had given her on her fifteenth birthday to put in her golden hair.

Though he swore to marry her, he never followed through. Yet a little boy was soon born of their love, and his light step and joyful laugh were heard echoing through the sunlit Tangiers villa of the wealthy traveler. And, one day—although the women of her family did tell her that a woman should never trust a man, that a man will always leave once he has gotten what he needed and wanted from a woman, that he would only remain if he must, if he had a ring around his finger, or nowhere else to be—one day, he left them, returned to his northern country and that other life that must have been patiently waiting for him all along.

Tangiers, which was a small town really, bristled with rumors of them, picked their lives apart with glee and flourish. It was said that the woman's white lace *mantilla* and the mother-of-pearl *peineta* whose elegance and timelessness drove them ill with envy, had turned a raven black the day the traveler left her and their little boy. It was also said that her golden hair turned gray and thin, and that she lost her mind. But she had always been a little mad; a woman doesn't fall like that for a man, a traveler, if she's not slightly mad to begin with, and so then his departure becomes a pretext for her final break. The crack had always been there, inside her absolute submission to him, inside the love she had given him. Now, the little boy, fruit of her embittered hope and love, would follow her around, a small, quiet shadow, and his laugh and quick feet would never be heard again.

This child had grown up in the traveler's, his father's, villa. He never lacked anything, for it was said his father had never quite forgotten his North African son, that he had recognized him as his own, even though he never wished to see him again. He had grown up sheltered from need, except for the deep, throbbing hunger for his father. He had never left the villa, even as an adult man, even after his mother's passing. It had always been his home. Aya would come to envy that.

He was now in his sixties, a famous local artist, who walked softly around his neighborhood with a German Shepherd at his side. A man who kept his overseas connections and whose heart, they said, was good.

A man who, one day, knocked at the Danes' door and asked the mother if this was the home of one Miss Aya Dane. The mother, at a loss, called the father.

Aya heard his soft, hesitant voice from her father's overcrowded office that was now her room. She opened the door. Her father's straight back and her mother's tall, opulent figure hid the caller from view; but she didn't need to see who it was. She had known that he would come.

twenty-five

Aya opened her eyes to find herself lying on the studio floor. Night had fallen, revealing the acute whiteness outside. She turned on the lights and wrapped her arms around her waist. She could feel the bones and the flatness beneath her skin. Kareem was gone. She felt feverish, panicked. She hadn't eaten properly in days. She went into the kitchen and prepared a sandwich. She devoured it and immediately made another one. Aya was not used to eating much. A couple of bites, a single meal, were enough to get her through the day. She could go days without eating more than a handful of nuts, or a single piece of fruit.

Her connections to the world at large were distended, strained to their breaking point. She could barely remember the time when she still believed there could be a place for her because she had grit and talent, and because that was the Dream people dreamed in this land.

Only Ari remained. Time was running out and he would be here soon. In less than a week, Aya had to turn over her painting to him.

She crossed the glass panels into the studio, turned on the light, walked toward the long back window that overlooked the street. The last full moon before the winter solstice had only just passed, and the lights of the stars had returned to the sky. And these very stars began talking to the voices in her head, in pleasurable conversation. She pulled open the curtains and the silvery whiteness of the snow and of the city lights poured in.

While Aya preferred working in the early dawn, there was something strangely satisfying, as she was nearing the completion of her painting, to work in the diffuse glow of half-moon, babbling stars and city lights.

As she stood in front of the painting, she felt a heat, a trepidation, exuding from it. It was waiting to be touched, shaped, finished, perhaps finally put to rest.

She began mixing the paints and oils. She touched the painting with her fingertips and felt its surface rise at her touch. Her fingers tingled and her blood ran warm. The paint on her fingertips glowed softly in the cool, clean night. It extended in slender rivulets up her hands like so many delicate tattoos.

She plunged her hands into the canvas. She thickened its surface with the heavy paints. She deepened its shadows, thinned the lines that needed thinning and enhanced those that needed to be enhanced. She relinquished her will. She bent down. The colors intensified as they touched the canvas, as though filled with a life of their own. They rose like waves when the storm hits the calm sea. They spread and glistened like foam when the storm hits full force. The blues, grays and whites of the tormented sea spread beneath the dark blue and black of a low, hovering sky.

She continued to paint. Her hands, arms and face were wet and dripping, and still she continued. When brushes unleashed and broke, her fingers groped around for new ones.

She couldn't explain the urgency she felt. The work both emanated from her and eluded her. The painting no longer simply submitted to her, or merged with her, becoming one with her. It now appeared to act of its own accord.

It—she wanted to call it *she*—had acquired its own mysterious purpose, one that no longer depended on her, that wished to escape her.

The storm suddenly subsided. The colors lay low, as did the horizon beyond the blue sea. They settled into a near-religious serenity, delicate, ephemeral. The brush itself became light as a feather, between her fingertips. It flew above the canvas, like birds rising above the dying sun. It brushed gently, tenderly, lovingly upon the softened surface of the canvas. The waves lay down, revealing the calmness of the sea, the limpidity of the horizon, the land that, surely, lay beyond.

The sea had taken many bodies into its abyss. Its golden-blue surface was tinged with darkness. It was a sea of loss. It held prisoner those who looked for passage without permission. It crushed hope in an instant and precipitated forgetfulness. And still they try the crossing in the hopes that maybe they'll be one of the lucky ones, one of those who sets foot on the shore on the other side. One of those who proves, even for a brief moment, that frontiers are in and of the mind. A pilgrim who finds sanctuary, a migrant whose journey ends. There, for the chosen ones, is the reward; there, beyond the sea, is the giving land.

No one ever wondered what reaching the other shore would be like. Or perhaps no one dared dream beyond the passage. The dream was wrapped up in the excruciating desire of departure and arrival. Beyond, was a mystery shrouded in words gleaned here and there, fragments of stories, or fantasies.

For those, like her, who experienced the release of arrival, there is shame in admitting loss and sadness at what was left behind. For those, like her, who managed to inscribe their ambition, their will, their talent upon this new world, this shame is even greater. For, in the end, it is a part of them that is left behind and must be recreated anew, amid magic tricks, double mirrors and pretenses of joy.

Aya read in an obscure book that people once died of homesickness. They called it nostalgia: the state of yearning for a past that cannot be retrieved or put to rest. Nostalgia, or homesickness, was a fatal disease but it was also the stuff of stories and poems. There was no shame in being homesick, in craving a return to lost roots. There was even a certain kind of pleasure, when it did not descend into madness and death, in conjuring fragments of the past, from stories gleaned here and there, from scents and family pictures, from music and, ultimately, from color.

But today, she couldn't dwell on such half-lights. She couldn't say that nostalgia was her way of being in the world. She couldn't say that her homesickness, even though she didn't know where home was anymore, was emptying her out. She couldn't say that her yearning for an imagined, past belonging was her exile, and it was condemning her to restless wanderings.

The world she now lived in was a world where she couldn't admit to such a state of mind, where it was a weakness. The world she now inhabited was one where movement, quickness, strength, staying ahead, maintaining the sheer-thin glow of perfect appearances, and killing pain and difference with overmedication was the new religion.

She also read, in her rare, quiet time, when the noise in her head subsided and the fireplace burned warm and kind, that this state of being at home and wanting to be at home is called "homefulness." This word no longer exists, as though the fullness of feeling it describes had also ceased to exist. She didn't know why words like these disappear, why they die, or who buries them.

There's a sense of failure associated with being content, being thankful for being at home. It's possible that the world may change once again and that there will be value in wanting to be at home and sadness in being far from home. But it would never be so for Aya. She would never have that fullness of feeling, for she had no home to return to. All she had left was herself, her work, her talent, Ari's commission and her pain—the incessant, excruciating ache in her head, limbs and stomach, which refused to be killed and which, for some reason, she couldn't let die.

Sprawled on the canvas, the work demanded her full attention, her allegiance, her submission. As she stood looking at it, its power over her grew; it felt more alive than she. The brush in her hand passed over its surface. The shapes and colors began to shift, swirl, arranging themselves into patterns and hues she hadn't intended or imagined. The waves rose and beckoned as though asking her to witness an event, a shipwreck, a forgotten story. The painting called her in, bringing her closer and closer into its depths. She felt it rise and open.

Her brush quivered, her hand stopped. She peered into the painting and saw neither sea, nor storm, nor land. Her intent had escaped her. The pain again seared through her body, nesting itself in her head, branding her, sending her reeling. She leaned on the canvas and waited for the pain to ebb. She felt, for the first time, a singular power emanating from the painting. The colors, the lines, the shapes seemed to resonate with their own purpose. Its pull on her had grown, and she no longer knew who controlled whom.

What did the painting want from her?

She put her hands on either side of her eyes and peered into it.

twenty-six

Aya's school was up in arms. It was preparing for an important visit. It bustled and buzzed in ways that made even its students eager. The walls and classrooms were washed, the bathrooms, in disrepair, were repainted a bright pink, a color that was cheap for lack of demand, and the broken doorknobs replaced by brand new ones that got the girls excited and giggling. The courtyard was decked with red and green lights, and colorful flags. Finally, as though worried that the students were not good enough for the whitewashed school, the administration advised them to be immaculately clean and properly dressed the day of the visit: to put their best shoes on, not the dirty slippers they liked to wear on a regular day and splash around in, and tie their hair in a neat ponytail, or, preferably, a well-adjusted veil. An important man was coming to see *their school*. Much-needed funds might be distributed, perhaps even directly into the headmistress's hands.

Aya's school—now a state-owned all-girls school dedicated to the production of fear and obedience—was founded in 1950 by James Stirling, a famous American poet and heir to a considerable fortune, as only Americans knew how to amass.

James Stirling had arrived in Tangiers after having his heart broken by the love of his life. He had met this love in the city of Paris and had quickly fallen under her charm. He wrote poems for her, and about her. Critics said they were some of his worst, and his readers shook their heads at the tragedy of another great voice surrendering to love.

Stirling did not see, at first, that his love was not fully reciprocated. He had opened up his arms, his heart and his considerable fortune to a woman who had seduced him with her sophistication and charm. Her red mouth smiled, while her restless eyes told stories of other places, other desires.

When Stirling's heart finally broke, he packed his bags and left Paris. The scent of her perfume, which permeated its streets and followed him everywhere he went, had become intolerable. He fled to Tangiers, promising himself he would never fall in love again. But he was wrong, and he did.

Stories have it that he fell in love with Tangiers itself. With its white streets and green tiles, its high hills and vertiginous falls into the blue-white of the sea. With its wild parties and unfettered artists. With its unparalleled feel of a new world in an ancient civilization.

But Stirling, like all true poets, had a tender heart. He began to see past the glitter and glamor into the actual shape of the city and its true inhabitants, those who had been born there and had grown up there. He walked deep into the city, taking in the rare perfume of a *medina* in the morning. The warm bread, the mint tea, the excited children, sugar from a hurriedly eaten breakfast still on their cheeks, the shrewd carpet seller and the loud-mouthed fish vendor with the gold earrings and imposing behind. Stirling also saw how thin some of these children were, how tired the fish vendor was, how worried the carpet seller. He looked past their persons and saw what expats who refuse to turn native, or even immigrant, can't see: the broken-down services, the dilapidated schools and insufficient hospitals.

Expats do not have a real claim on the city of their choosing, nor do they care to have one. They are the traveling strangers, the privileged elite whose true wealth resides in their detachment, in the ties they are not obliged to honor. They are the fake gold that the powerful shower on their dominion. They are here, for a time only, eager to fulfill a mission, perhaps write a book or close a deal. Their goal, in their short time here, is to be integrated into the expat circles and enjoy their special status as privileged foreigners. But sometimes, they slip.

What was happening to Stirling was the following. He was transforming from an expatriate into an immigrant. And like all immigrants, he needed to place his mark on the city of his choosing. Unlike most immigrants, it would be easier for him to do so.

Because he was a successful, forward-looking American poet who had survived even a failed love affair in the City of Lights, he knew he must contribute to his newfound city's progress.

After many long months and lengthy negotiations, he finally convinced the city to support his project. That was how the poet founded the first all-girls school in Tangiers, the one Aya now studied in. At least, that was the buzz around town.

Stirling never married. He was, however, rumored to have had a son with a Jewish Moroccan woman, who looked after the villa he owned in the Tangiers hills. It was said the three of them led a quiet, happy life for a while in the beautiful villa Stirling owned, far from both his and her communities. It came as a surprise, then, when Stirling suddenly picked up and left the city to return to the United States, a country he had left over twenty years ago. He left Tangiers the very year it lost its international status and returned to the Moroccan state.

He left the house and a sizable amount of money to his housekeeper and her son. He also recognized the boy as his own. All that he asked in return was for his son, when he reached his twenty-first birthday, to take care of the school he had built.

The child, in the manner of the Spaniards, who the people of Tangiers feel so close to, decided to carry both his father's and his mother's names. He was Michel Abensour Stirling: Abensour, after his mother, Rachel Abensour, and Stirling, after his father, James Stirling.

James Stirling left and never returned to Tangiers. Nor did he, usually so tenderhearted, ever inquire about the son or the woman he had left behind.

———

Michel Abensour Stirling was tall and thin like his father. But he had the piercing blue eyes and red-gold hair of his mother—a legacy of the Visigoths, a barbaric northern tribe who had conquered her land many centuries ago. He spoke English, Spanish, some Arabic, Berber and Hakitiya, the Judeo-Spanish dialect once spoken by the Jews of northern Morocco.

His mother died when Michel was twenty-one, thirteen years after James Stirling's departure. Throughout those years, she had not married, nor had she ever had any other child. She took care of her son and of the house her American lover had left her. She waited for James Stirling to return, or to inquire about her and their son, but he never did. Then she waited for her son to turn twenty-one, to become a man, to finally let death enter the gates.

Upon her deathbed, she took her son's hand and asked for his forgiveness. "When the heart of a true Tangiers woman is broken, she does not survive it."

And so, Michel, who spoke many languages and whose ancestry was glorious and diversified, found himself alone, with no one to converse with or to share his vast knowledge with. When he became an old man, he acquired a German Shepherd to chase away indigenous wanderers and dirty children from his high gates, white walls and blue-tiled overhangs.

He was a very different man from the one his father was. He let the city close in on him and very rarely left his villa on the high, quiet hills of Tangiers. He was not a poet nor did he have a tender heart, as people thought. When he was a child, he may have had a tender heart. But when his father left him and his mother to their fates in the great old villa, something inside him shattered and he was never whole again.

Michel did not take care of the school nor did he honor his father's will to maintain it. As the city returned to the Moroccan state, so did the school. At least, those were the stories the Tangerine had heard.

This story mattered to the school and its administration—and to Aya—because the visitor they were all waiting for, and getting clean for, was Michel Abensour Stirling.

At first, they didn't know who Michel Abensour Stirling was, nor did the administration remember who James Stirling was. Though his name was placarded in gold letters on the front of the school, no one had ever bothered to read the plaque. A double phone call from the US embassy and the Moroccan Ministry of Foreign Affairs convinced the administration of the historical, and hopefully present-day, importance of this guest and advised the school to welcome him with open arms and a respectable façade.

This story mattered to Aya, because Abensour Stirling was the cold, ageing expat who had chased her away from his property in the high hills of Tangiers with the assistance of his German Shepherd.

According to Michel Abensour Stirling himself, when he had chased her away that day and seen the expression in her eyes before she turned and fled, he was seized with an immense anger. Something in Aya's eyes reminded him of himself the day he woke up to find his father had gone. It was an undecipherable mixture of shame, confusion and fear. It was the child blaming itself for being abandoned, or hit, humiliated or otherwise hurt. It was the expression of lost innocence.

In time, Abensour Stirling's anger dissipated and made way for a feeling he hadn't allowed himself to feel in a long time, not even after his mother's death: sadness. He couldn't chase from his memory the image of that young girl running away from him and Buck, his half-sane German Shepherd. He waited for the memory to dissipate, but it only became more powerful, penetrating his dreams, interrupting his early morning walks by the beach, flashing onto his bathroom mirror as he stood in front of it, shaving his thin face.

After many months had passed, he decided to look for the girl, and find a way to eradicate the memory. He asked about her to the men guarding the villas on his street, promising them a fair reward if anyone could tell him who the girl was. Because this was Tangiers, where news travels fast and secrets are burdens people take turns carrying, he finally found her. One of the guards told him what he knew. "*Sidi,* her name is Aya Dane. She lives with her parents and a brother in the neighborhood behind Petit Socco, in the Rue Cervantes. And, *Sidi*, this is a strange find. She's a student in the school your father founded, fifty-five years ago. Would you like me to take you to her?"

For many months, Abensour Stirling did not act on this knowledge. He was not a man of action, or great resolve. A little girl had disturbed the routine of his old age. She had trespassed into a part of Tangiers that should be beyond the reaches of the indigenes and the poor. She was the reminder of the young world that lay beyond his high gates. And of the disappointment that accompanied it. He had been a fool to believe that looking for the child could bring anything good. There was no magic left in the world; not when your father up and leaves you one morning, when you are eight years old and need him the most.

James Stirling had tried to contact his son, once, after his mother's death. He had sent him a short letter inviting him to come stay with him in Philadelphia, where he was currently based. Michel had never replied nor gone to visit him. It was not clear whether he had ever read the letter, for it had remained, imperfectly sealed, in a box on his desk for all those years.

After many months of inactivity, Michel Abensour Stirling got up, went into his father's study, which was now his study, and opened a leather-bound address book that had belonged to his father and which his mother, and then he, regularly updated.

He looked for the private number of the American Consul to Tangiers and dialed the number. It was not long before he had the Consul at the end of the line.

A few days later, Abensour Stirling got out of bed and rang for service. His room was a chiaroscuro created by the lattices of the wooden windows. He fed his German Shepherd, sat at the breakfast table placed in the bedroom veranda, had a meal of black coffee, fresh-squeezed orange juice and farm-churned butter. He then went into the dressing room and chose white linen pants and a gray shirt that had been left behind by his father. He wore brown moccasins and a white Panama hat that had also belonged to his father, and that were a little big for him. He was—for the first time since his mother had passed—expected somewhere.

The 1970s water-green Mercedes was waiting for him at the door. The driver, Mustapha, was holding the back door open. Abensour Stirling sat in the back seat and, for the first time in many years, breathed in the musky scent of the leather seats. The American Consul of Tangiers and the highest representative of the Moroccan foreign ministry in the city were waiting for him.

———

In the meantime, on the other side of town, Aya's school was as decked and ready as a bride on her wedding day. Aya and her classmates had been asked to form two rows between the school gates and the main school building. They were given Moroccan and American flags to hold and wave when the gates opened and the cars passed through. They were then told to go into their classrooms and wait for the important visitors to come see their classrooms and their work. They were reminded to be on their best behavior and to remember how graced they were by such an important visit.

They, the poor, blessed schoolchildren, watched as the fancy cars entered through their crumbling gates. Most of the students had their eyes wide open, and those who could, tried to peer inside the cars, smiling at their distorted faces reflected in the dark windows. Finally, a dilapidated Mercedes, green like the moors in the springtime, rolled sputtering in.

Aya was sitting at her desk when the headmistress came to get her. Word had it that the officials and the quiet gentleman at their side had asked to see their best students. This may or may not have been true. She was not one of those selected. So it came as a great surprise when the headmistress herself, tight-lipped, came back for her.

"They want to see you. Why? Do you know that man from somewhere? Why the sudden interest?"

Aya sensed her anger and remained quiet, waiting for the storm to pass.

"Have you misbehaved, like the others? Whore…"

She spat her guile and hatred, but Aya remained quiet and still. That was what hunted animals instinctively know to do.

What Aya did sense was that something was about to happen. Something that seemed to profoundly disturb the headmistress and that caused her to spit more venom than usual. And that could only be a good thing.

Chairs had been brought into the headmistress's office and placed in a circle in the middle of the room. Serious-looking men sat huddled in that circle of chairs, in the way of the elders of the mountains that surrounded Tangiers. Aya was ushered in, the serious-looking men turned in their seats to look at her. She stopped, frozen in her tracks. She had recognized one of them.

It was *him*—the man who had haunted her nightmares, who had thrown his dog at her when she was running away from him. The man whose words had cut through her and whose scorn bit at her beyond the days and the nights. She backed away into the headmistress's white and black-garbed body. There was hardness all around her. There was also, she sensed, a soft presence in the corner of the large room. But it was too far, too vague, and Aya felt trapped by the tall, hard bodies surrounding her.

Michel Abensour Stirling saw the look in her eyes, the same look that had taken him away from his life of bitterness and anger, from his violent slumber. The look that had haunted him and that he had come to crave secretly, for, he would tell her many years later, it reminded him of another look, another child, whom he thought he had long since buried, alongside his mother and his father.

He rose to greet her. He spoke to her in Arabic, articulating carefully, looking for his words. His accent was not one Aya had heard before. Singsong and clipped, it was the local Jewish accent he had inherited from his mother and her traditions.

She listened, at first startled and confused, before finally understanding. This was an apology. He asked her about her schoolwork, her interests. He asked if he could take an interest in her, help her in any way, guide her. As he spoke, Aya realized that he wasn't simply apologizing to her. He was apologizing to the city, to the school, to the people surrounding him, to himself, to his mother, in his name and also in his father's name. What a peculiar man, who suddenly opens up to the world and finds that he can only offer his guilt and regret.

To the great disappointment of the school and the officials of the two countries, he did not offer anything else. He did not offer funds for the rehabilitation of the school. He did not offer scholarships or the renovation of the fifty-year-old bathroom stalls. He offered nothing. He had not come to give the school hope or a fresh start; he came, simply, to see

Aya Dane. The rest was not his concern. He was not a man of the people, nor a man versed in charitable donations, not a man mindful of the connections between the world and himself.

Michel Abensour Stirling would later tell her that *she* was his hope. She was what was left of the school, of the promise he never believed he needed to honor, and of the child inside him that he wished to lay to rest forever. He had come to be saved, not to save.

That was why, when Aya was dismissed from the head-mistress's office, and though he himself didn't understand this, Abensour Stirling did not feel the contentment he thought he would feel. He felt like an old, a very old, man who had let his life slip away from him without even trying to steer it in the right direction.

He needed to do more.

As he left the school a teacher approached him. She had understood, better and faster than everyone else, that this man was not made of the stuff of saviors, that he was not a generous or giving man. This teacher saw that he barely had the strength to walk into the school. She knew he would not save them and that they would all be left to their fates. But she could do something. She could save one of them. She could save one and watch countless others drown.

She could let the sweet girl whose dream was to save all the stray dogs in the city, go down. She could let the rebel, in whose nature it was to question everything, go down. She could let the philosopher, who instinctively knew there was a wrong and a right, go down. She could let all the others, including herself, whose dedication and passion as a teacher few had seen or would ever notice, go down in the murky waters of a failed system. But she could save one.

And that was probably as it should be, as the God above, if indeed he was there and indeed watched and cared, may have intended. For the one she would help save was the very one whom she had advised to leave Tangiers and never look back, and the very one Michel Abensour Stirling had asked for in the headmistress's office. She knew this because she, too, had been in the headmistress's office, though none of the gentlemen had noticed her, for the headmistress needed her comforting presence by her side, in difficult or trying times.

As Abensour Stirling was about to climb back into his vehicle, she touched his arm and, in a low, urgent voice, told him what he needed to know about Aya Dane. He turned slowly to face the small, nondescript woman whom he would never have noticed, but whose determination was a thing of heaven, something akin to the work of angels, and that, even he, with his cynicism, could see; and a smile lit his dead eyes.

Years later, when his own memory was about to fail him, and the past mangled his present, Abensour Stirling would tell Aya about these events, and how he came to find her and adopt her, even made her an American, he said proudly, after her parents' disappearance. He walked her through the meanders of his fumbling memories, took her through the dark alleyways and closed doors of his mind, which frightened him so, and into his brief moments of joy. And through it all, even at her young age, she saw, better than he, what he was desperately trying to remember, to touch, what he was trying to find, and that he never would.

Aya didn't know if Abensour Stirling ever understood that his entire life was a plea, a prayer, an embarrassed yearning, for the return of a precious loss. For the return of a father who, he had always known—but how could he relinquish that hope?—had consciously, selfishly left him and would never come back for him. That was why Abensour Stirling had had such a slow, uneventful life: he had relinquished everything else, surrendered fully and totally to the passing of time and the feeling of abandonment, agreed to live in the decrepit house where his father's and his mother's love had come to die, and actively, day after day, turned it into his own mausoleum.

Yet, with that peculiar sense of honor that sometimes inhabited his acts, he didn't create villains or heroes to validate the choices he made or the long, quasi-centennial inertia that characterized his existence. He allowed the grayness to settle in, and the accompanying rot to form.

twenty-seven

A tall, slightly stooped man stood at the door. There was something of a hawk about him. He spoke French with a strong English accent, with a touch of Hakiti sunshine and a hint of song.

"Is Miss Aya Dane here?"

Her mother stood at the door, looking in stunned silence at this man from another Tangiers. Not knowing what to do or how to answer him, she called for her husband. He approached, and the strange old man asked again.

"I'm sorry to come to your home without warning. I would like to see your daughter, Miss Aya Dane."

"Why are you looking for our daughter?"

"If I may come in and explain to you...It's a long story."

The parents glanced wearily inside, as though their home held a beast they hid from the world. Aya's mother finally made a decision. She stepped aside.

"Of course, please come in. I will tell Aya."

As the two men sat on the threadbare couch in the narrow salon, Aya's mother went to the kitchen and prepared the tea, in the manner of her own mother, and of her mother before her. Aya came in to watch, and her mother glanced at her.

"There is a man come here to see you. A *European*. Old."

"Yes, Mother."

Her mother was quiet. Suddenly, she poured the hot water into the sink, a gesture believed to anger the genies living below ground, but the mother, usually so careful, didn't seem to care anymore, and threw the tea grains on the kitchen table. She wiped her hands on her long skirt and held Aya's face in her hands. There was a rare tenderness, an ominous kindness, in the way she held her daughter, in the way her eyes brushed all over her, like an artist lovingly cradling her work, before the buyer comes for it. Aya should have understood then what would happen, but she was too young, perhaps, or too naïve. Her mother spread the tea grains, the mint leaves and the sugar in front of them. When she spoke, her voice was cool and strong, and it comforted Aya.

"Come, child. It's time you learn how tea is made, in the way of the women in your family. Of your grandmother and of your great-grandmother, who received the knowledge directly from the great Arab traveler who brought back the Chinese tea with him to Tangiers."

She smiled, and Aya didn't know if this tale was true or if, like many other stories with clear beginnings and ends, it was a myth. As she worked, she spoke.

"What does he want? What have you done?"

"Nothing impure, mother."

"Am I supposed to believe that…after your brother…"

Aya fixed her eyes on her mother's mechanical gestures. She imagined them as they once were, filled with love, her delicate fingers sprinkling the tea grains like seeds of happiness over the hot water and adding sugar like one adds sweetness to the bitterness of life. But the mother's tea no longer tasted sweet, nor did it bring warmth to its drinker. When her mother raised her eyes to Aya, they were inquisitive.

"Who is this man, Aya? He speaks in a way I haven't heard in many years, ever since I was a child."

"He came to my school. His father, he says, founded my school. And his name is Michel Abensour Stirling."

Aya couldn't tell her mother the entire truth. Her mother said, "When I was a child, many people spoke with that accent, with that lilt. It is strange: he is both foreign and one of us, a European and a son of the land. And that name, Abensour, he cannot deny it's one of ours, even though all of those who carried the name are gone. To the Middle East, Canada, France. Except him. So, who is that man sitting in our living room? Ask him, Aya."

Aya nodded.

Abensour Stirling had a peculiar way of expressing himself. The roughness and cruelty of his words a few months ago, which chased her away from the lush bougainvillea alleys of the Tangiers hills, still rang in her ears. It seemed to her that this was a man who had kept silent for the greater part of his life. He must have used his voice only to scream and scare away other trespassers.

Aya glanced at her brother's room. His door was closed and no sound came from the room. Kareem might well let them be this evening.

She and her mother returned to the living room carrying trays of tea and sweets. They placed the trays in front of the two men, and her father served the tea. Abensour Stirling took the tea and sweets and, in his words and voice from another time, explained his presence.

"I am here in the reinstated tradition of my father, the great Philadelphian poet James Stirling, and of my mother, Rachel Abensour, of the Abensours of Tangiers, Sebta, Canada and India. Thus, I am here, filled with guilt and looking for atonement. My father founded the school where your daughter studies, in 1950, when Tangiers was the glorious international city we hear so much about, and know, paradoxically, so little about. I have lived in Tangiers my entire life but haven't been to the school since I was a small child. Too painful? I do not know. I met your daughter, by accident, a few months past. I saw her in my street. She seemed happy. She skipped about while she ate her warm, sweet peanuts and explored my alleyway. I knew that look. I am ashamed to admit that I resented her happiness, her *insouciance*. Do you know, I don't recall…Well, but that's of no interest to you, I can see that. I believe my dog and I may have scared her away. I would like to make it up to you, if I may. I have a plan."

Until the last sentence, Aya could see her mother and father were confused, trying to piece events into chronologies, to tell apart the truth from the falsehoods or omissions. When Abensour Stirling finished, however, there was a tension in her mother's back and a stiffness in her father's hands. Her father said:

"Is this true, Aya?"

She nodded.

"Why are you here today, Sir?" the mother then asked.

"I am here to make amends. To atone, to straighten crooked lines. Too many broken things, alas."

A door opened behind them. No one heard it open or saw the young man who was now listening, his back to the wall, his arms across his chest.

Aya stared at the family portrait in the living room. This portrait reminded her that she was part of something important: a family. That she had roots and a belonging. She had a safe haven from which to step into the world and which would protect her when its trials became too harsh. She was Aya Dane.

In the portrait, her parents were young, and Kareem and Aya were children. It was a simple picture that had everyone stare candidly into the camera, smiling and at ease. Kareem and Aya were seated in the foreground, while their parents stood behind them. She had always harnessed strength from it.

When Aya saw Abensour Stirling at her door, she understood that her life was on the brink of an irreversible change. He walked in like a breeze from the north. He smelled of wealth and privilege, of a nonchalance that proudly bore its recklessness toward others. He was a reminder of a world where people remained where they were or left by choice, not by force. His passport allowed him to cross seas and continents at a whim. He could, if he so pleased, fly over the Atlantic or cruise through the Mediterranean without having to see his neighbors drowning and their wooden boats capsizing, or be overly concerned that half of those swallowed by the sea were children. That too was terrifying for the likes of Aya.

And so, of course, with that tremendous power that was his as an American passport holder, Abensour Stirling did not see the need to leave the crumbling city of Tangiers. His dreams were at peace and his cravings lay in his past, not in the future.

Aya passed by the portrait and touched it with her fingertips. She closed her eyes and took her time. When she opened them, she saw something in it that she hadn't before. Her parents were not protective walls around her and her brother. They hovered in the background, and their arms hung loosely at their sides. They didn't embrace their children, as Aya always assumed they did. Their eyes were lightless and anxious. They were detached from one another, as they were detached from them, their children. As for Kareem, the sadness was already there. It was in the grim lines of his mouth and the clenched bones of his jaw. Kareem must have known about his parents' detachment, and the reason for it. As for Aya, she faced the camera, straight, unblinking, already separated from her family, but too young to see it. It was as though they all shared a secret among themselves, and only she had been left out in the dark.

She looked up from the photograph to find Kareem looking at her. There was no anger or scorn in his eyes, as there had been these last months, only pity. Yes, he felt pity for her. Why would he pity her?

Their father's voice cut into the silence like a knife.

"What do you mean by that, Mr. Stirling?"

"Mr. *Abensour* Stirling…I mean, I would like to make amends. I have been to Aya's school, I have spoken to her teachers, and one was particularly helpful. I have inquired about your situation…"

"What gives you the right…?"

"Please, sir, hear me out. I understand from one of her teachers that Aya has a difficult situation at home."

Her father rose, his face closed, his fist clenched. But her mother put her hand on his arm and told him to sit down. Aya's gaze returned to the family portrait in the living room. Things were not what they seemed. And her suspicion that she had been kept in the dark was steadily growing. They were hiding something from her.

Abensour Stirling continued. "I assure you there is no need to take offense. I have a debt toward your daughter, and I believe it is in my power to help her."

Her mother asked, "What are you saying, Mr. Abensour? What is this debt you wish to acquit yourself of?"

"...I am saying that I know the difficulties you are facing. The prolonged unemployment, the other child, a son, I'm told. I can take Aya, raise her like my own daughter. She has a few years left before she graduates. I will give her the best there is."

"And in exchange? Do you wish her to be your wife?"

"Dear Madam, I am not interested in a wife. Perchance a companion. A friend. My offer is an innocent one. I'm an American citizen. A wealthy one, as you may have heard. I will make it legal. I will adopt Aya. She will be an American citizen...That's my offer."

"You're making a mistake. We do not give our daughters away, just like that, just because we've fallen on hard times, because we're born on the wrong side of the world."

"She won't be a prisoner. Quite the opposite, I'll be opening doors for her."

The parents were silent, and so was Aya.

She was back in the meandering alleys of old Tangiers, chased by a dog and a man. The dog had caught up with her and bitten her leg. The pain was deep and the skin broken. The man had watched as she lay bleeding on the ground. He held his dog at bay and spat on the ground near her head, before returning to his dark blue alley, to his dark blue door and his dark blue life.

Kareem was suddenly in front of Aya. The expression on his face was undecipherable. She backed away from him, from his barely restrained anger and his hatred. His mother looked at him long and hard, filled with emotions and truths she could not share with anyone. The truth was, mothers didn't know how to raise their sons. The truth was, mothers made their sons violent and fearful. They filled them with a power they could never release and a pride that would gnaw at their insides. She thought of how mothers played with their sons to ease the pain of weak or hateful or absent husbands, of their own weakness, their subjection. She thought of how Kareem had become a reflection of her darkest, deepest failures.

The mother rose and went into Aya's room. A few minutes later, she came back with a suitcase and backpack.

"Take her with you. Here are her belongings. Take care of her."

Aya couldn't look at her mother. She didn't understand the sudden harshness in her voice, but she couldn't deny hearing it. She tried to wrap her mind around her mother's words but found a sinking darkness instead. She backed away, her heart pounding.

Desperate for an answer, Aya stared once again at the family portrait. She saw how the grayness faded into shades and shadows, dotted by reds and oranges so intense they hurt the eye. It was as though the photograph had been left too long under the sun and its delicate surface had been burnt. She wished it could have been burnt thoroughly, the faces and memories utterly devoured by the sun. She wished it could all burn to the ground and ease her pain. She turned to her father, waiting for him to say something, to turn the man away, to say that he needed her, that families were unbreakable, that love was stronger than adversity. But her father was thinking of different things.

He was thinking of the unspeakable evil that had taken place under his roof and the even more unbearable evil that lay outside its doors. He was thinking of his helplessness and his inability to protect his daughter, his wife, his son. What was left of a man in this country, in this city of theirs? Where had all the men gone? And what would happen to the women and children they had left behind?

He looked at Aya, and she saw that his resolve had already crumbled, that shame would be the only surviving emotion in her father's heart.

"Make sure she forgets where she is from," said her father before lowering his head and returning to his bedroom. Aya heard her parents' bedroom door close and felt a sadness she had never felt before. She looked at her mother and saw that the light and warmth in her eyes had been extinguished. In their stead was a coldness, a roughness Aya didn't think she could survive. She nodded and asked to go to her room to fetch one last item.

She went to her room and rummaged through her old toys until she found it. The doll, her muñeca. She held it against her. She heard her name being called and turned to find her mother standing in the doorway.

The mother closed the door behind her with her right hand. In her left, she held the photograph. "You were looking at this picture. Why?"

Aya kept quiet. Would those be the last words she would hear before leaving her home? Her mother sat on the bed, her hands folded around the silver frame. She said:

"I have a story to tell you."

"You, who could never tell me a story?"

"I, who was never good at telling you stories, who could only touch your hair and wait for you to sleep, I have a story to tell you. A story no mother should tell her daughter, but one which you must now hear."

That is when it happened, when colors replaced words, when sensations replaced thoughts. Her mother spoke, and a swirl of colors clouded Aya's thoughts, blinded her.

"It happened," she said, "at the beach. It was a perfect day. Blue sky, gold sand, a crisp wind and gentle waves. You were holding your little red muñeca, and your brother was dressed in his football jersey, the green-and-yellow one he was so proud of, his orange ball in his arms."

She stared at the photograph in her hands long enough to let the bitterness through.

"This beach, beautiful and quiet, had its own darkness: a part of it was forbidden to the general public. And beyond the beach, a palace. It belonged to a foreign prince, and we were not allowed in. And between the beach and the palace, a forest of shrubbery and planted trees. You didn't know, you were too small. Before we could stop you, you had skipped over onto the private beach, the doll still in your arms. Kareem ran after you to bring you back, but it was too late, you had already crossed over the limit. Two armed guards appeared and began pushing you and your brother around. Do you remember any of this?"

Loud voices, brutal chins, steely eyes. Aya shook her head at the inconsistency of the memory, at the very real possibility that she had created it from thin air to ease her mother's own grief.

"Your father and I came to your rescue, to explain that you were only children playing, that you meant no harm."

The words and the pain floated into the air. It was hard for Aya to listen, and she wished her mother would stop.

"The armed guards wouldn't listen. They threatened us. A third guard came. He was not in his normal state…drunk, on drugs, out of his mind. His eyes were red and his speech was slurred. He dragged me away from the others, into the bushes. There was nothing your father could do. The two guards told him to take the children, you and your brother, and wait.

"At last night fell, and they let me go."

———————

Night had fallen. And this story, which Aya had been a part of, at whose heart she was, and which she didn't remember, was now only furious color and swirling shade.

"Why don't I remember?"

"You were too young. Your father and Kareem shielded you."

"Shielded me? What about you? Why did no one shield you?"

"Choices have to be made, beloved. Reasonable choices are a luxury in wild, unbearable times."

"And Kareem remembers?"

"Yes. He remembered everything. He spent the next nights curled up in his room, staring into the darkness. He never said anything to us, just as we never said anything to him. He was never the same after that. Perhaps that is why he is who he is now. But that is why you must go. Leave a home that cannot protect you. That is why we must agree to part with you, to let some stranger offer you shelter."

"You are punishing me now, for that day?"

The mother remained quiet. Her hands were shaking.

"Mother," Aya said, "why did you keep this from me? Why this secret? This lie? Don't you see, it has destroyed everything..."

"What was destroyed, was destroyed. We didn't mean to keep it a secret, nor did I mean to ever tell you what had happened that day at the beach, and why we never returned to the seashore. That happened on its own, in the way family secrets do. It started out of love for you, to protect you."

"It has destroyed us."

"It has destroyed us. But now you have a chance. And you must take it and never look back. We are your salt."

"You are my salt."

"You must go, beloved. We can't protect you, we can't help you, we have forgotten how to love. We have forgotten how to be brave. This is what is left of our courage. This is our last act of courage. Save yourself, for here the dust is settling in."

The mother came to Aya and embraced her. Her hands touched her face and hair. When she left the room, the father was waiting for her.

Aya could hear them.

"Did you tell her?"

"Yes."

"Did she remember?"

"Remember? Perhaps she doesn't even believe. But she understands. She will go. She understands fear now."

Aya looked around her room. The room. It felt like cardboard, thin and damp. A makeshift refuge that could no longer hold her. She walked out, the doll still held tightly against her chest, pressing against it.

She passed by her brother and felt his scorn, his rejection of her. She also felt something else, but she must have dreamt it, a dark, silent regret. That feeling soon passed. Without saying a word, he raised his hand and snatched the doll from her.

"Only children are allowed toys. You are now like all the others, spoiled and filthy. You are dead to me, and to us. Get out."

He spat on the ground near her feet. His words and his scorn cut deep, but they were, they had to be, of the past, just as now were the softness and the tenderness that had once been Aya's home: memories she would train herself to forget.

"I'm ready," she said, and followed a bowing Abensour Stirling out the door.

As she left her parents' home, she heard it. The music she hadn't heard since that day Kareem had pressed his need against her and the mother had denied her son's unbearable act and closed her eyes to the change in both her children. The day she saw her own aggressors reflected in her son but chose not to fight for her daughter. "Dance Me to the End of Love."

Aya wanted to run back in, to curl herself against her mother, in the warmth of her bed, to close her eyes and let her tell her the hurt would go away.

Why were they playing this song today and now? Was it relief for her departure? Was it in sadness or in joy? Was it to forget? Was it in memory of the life they could have had and were meant to have, if it had not been for the beach, if it had not been for the sea, if it had not been for the land? Was it in remembrance of the family they thought they once were, before the world walked into their home and broke their walls and their strength? Or because their lives were a dying dream that they refused to wake up from.

twenty-eight

My diary feels like sawdust between your fingers, does it not? Brittle and ashen, worn from within, from the touch of air, of light, of fingers turning pages. And you wonder if the words will stand till the very end. Your hands become light, your touch becomes soft, for you know that there is much you still don't understand, and that you must understand, before it's too late.

I felt the doorknob crumble as my fingers closed the door. I didn't need to look behind me to know that the door was also crumbling. All doors have crumbled behind me since. I don't need to look behind my shoulders anymore to know that everything I try to close, or am told to close, turns stiff and brittle, like salt, like sawdust, and falls to the floor.

He told me to come with him, and they said I should go. They closed the door, not I. They pretended that closed doors were opportunities, but I know better. That's why they crumble, that's why they don't do their job of keeping me inside, safe and warm, or protecting me from the outside, cold and dangerous. The doors I touch are not doors at all. They are the crumbling refuse of people's choices and determinations of my life, of the paths I should take. And so they can't hold.

You're at ease in your chair, which is my chair, for you think you are beginning to understand, to know, for you imagine you've begun to slip into my skin, look through my eyes, unlock my mechanism.

I left with him, because I was told to go, because he himself had broken down their— our—door, first. He had come into their lives and offered them a passageway they had never dreamed of. He had put in front of them a choice that is not one, a choice that is a dictate, a threat. And they had yielded. But the doors will never close behind them, just as they will never close behind him, or behind me.

One must not play with doorways, must not open and peek inside, for it's the edifice that's shaken.

That's why I build walls, not doors. I build walls around me that have no doorway. Wall after wall, layer upon layer, I run from the gathering dust and the looming shade.

That's why my canvases are filled with color and why they can explode into form, materialize into objects, into fragments, into stories. Because there are shapes beyond the straight lines of walls and the make-believe protection of doorways. And those shapes and colors will not crumble between my hands, will not betray me.

twenty-nine

The painting released her. The paintbrush between Aya's fingers was an extension of her pain. It elevated and transcribed it on the canvas. Or was it the other way around? There was a taste of ashes in her mouth.

She put down the paintbrush and held on to the canvas. It felt hot and powerful, burning her hands, like a fire that won't be extinguished. All around, the world was a formidable, banal, empty gray. And Aya…The pain had taken over her body, making it difficult to breathe, or even to stand. She had very little strength left.

She knew she couldn't keep going for much longer and that she urgently needed to finish the painting, but the past was gathering speed.

She picked up the paintbrush. It was heavy, expectant, as though already full of the colors that would soon be pressed upon the canvas. It trembled, or she trembled. She held it tighter, or it held her tighter. The delicate, brittle piece of wood between her fingers was heaving and unbalanced, like a fragile boat on turbulent waters. It could be split in two, shattered in a hundred pieces, in an instant. Just like her. But they had a purpose to fulfill and that purpose, this time, would not allow itself to be sunk to the bottom of a deep, dark ocean.

Aya gathered her fear and dread into a hardened knot at the back of her throat, close to the jugular, and started painting. As soon as the brush touched the canvas, the now familiar, blinding pain shot through her body, and she lost consciousness.

thirty

The door closed behind her, and she was now alone with the foreign gentleman whose presence at her side would never be a comforting one. How could she have known then that she would never see her family again?

Michel Abensour Stirling was himself just awakening to his life. He could not put himself in Aya's shoes nor could he understand her particular fears and confusion. That inability to understand another human being, or to feel genuine empathy, was Abensour Stirling's prime entanglement with the world. The only time he could recall feeling any empathy, or yearning, or tired sense of guilt, was when his dog had sunk his teeth in a little girl's leg. This peculiar feeling, this stilted sense of empathy, gnawed at him for several months, before he finally chose to find a remedy for it.

At first, Aya didn't know what the mild-mannered, absent-eyed gentleman expected of her. As time passed and he kept his promise of sending her to a private school, the only American school in Tangiers, and watching over her education, she began to believe in his story of redemption. He paid for her books and for her clothes. Aya now had shoes that didn't pinch her feet and well-adjusted outfits. But she had never felt as much a misfit or a fraud in her life.

The Tangiers American School was a school for diplomats' kids and wealthy locals. Aya never belonged. She felt like a poor girl disguised to look rich. She began to detach herself from what was happening to her, forcing shut her own inner turmoil. She knew this was a once in a lifetime opportunity that she couldn't squander, and so she gritted her teeth and rarely, if ever, floundered.

Abensour Stirling told her that this was her ticket to the United States. The United States, a place she knew nothing about except for two things: September 11 and—thanks to Miss Mai—Maryam Mirzakhani.

Maryam Mirzakhani was Miss Mai's hero. She was an Iranian mathematician whose picture she had plastered to her classroom wall. In the picture, which Miss Mai's girls stared at, wide-eyed, every day, she was a delicate young woman with cropped brown hair and sad, earnest eyes full of intelligence. Having left her native Tehran and her modest veil behind to make the United States her home, she was proof enough for Miss Mai, though she preferred when Maryam Mirzakhani wore the veil, that the US couldn't be a completely evil place. The devil had not finished work on his headquarters there yet, she would tell the girls, with a twinkle in her eye.

Maryam Mirzakhani was so young and carried such hope, such pride. And look, Miss Mai told the girls, proudly adjusting her own veil, with her short brown hair, her slender neck, her humble eyes, it was like Mirzakhani was still carrying the veil, the modesty, within. Born in Iran, she had found glory in the US before losing her battle against cancer. That was the fate of our Muslim brothers and sisters today, said Miss Mai: the world—even diseases—are against us.

Before Abensour Stirling told Aya about the US, that was all she knew: two broken towers that had spread dread across the world and a brilliant young Iranian woman, who died too soon.

He told her of his father's country, his city. He depicted extraordinary, colorful, improbable details, since he was feeding her tales of a country that he himself had never been to—more lore than fact. He painted for her the portrait of a land that harbored great institutions of higher learning, a land welcoming to all, if only they had the courage to work hard and the will to succeed. He reminded Aya that, as his adopted daughter, she had a claim to the American citizenship and he would help her go there if she found her way into one such institution. "Like Maryam Mirzakhani?" Aya would ask, and Abensour Stirling would laugh and reply, "Nonsense. Who is this person anyways? Another one of your occult visions?"

Sometimes, Abensour Stirling would peer into her eyes and smile shyly at her. "You are almost like me now, motherless, fatherless, in search of your soul." And when he would see how Aya fought to keep the tears from falling, he would tap her lightly on the head and, a strange satisfaction in his eyes, walk out of the room. And Aya would stay alone in her room, sometimes for entire days and nights.

———

One day, a few weeks after her arrival, and without any news of her family, she decided to approach Abensour Stirling and ask his permission to go see them.

She found him sitting in his living room, amid the dying tropical plants and the graying cacti vases, his shirt rolled high up on his thin elbows, his fingers painstakingly piecing together a broken ceramic plate.

This was one of his favorite hobbies. He spent long, lazy afternoon hours fixing broken objects for a modest fee. It was for his own enjoyment, never for the fee. It was a hobby that had come to him naturally, the answer to a lonely child's silent days.

He called it art. In the tight, neurotic world of expat collectors, he had made quite a name for himself. They would send him artifacts to piece together, repaint, reassemble. Aya watched him in silence. She stood in the doorway, hesitating to go inside. She thought that, despite his appearance and his claims, Abensour Stirling knew how to fix broken things, if he tried. Or perhaps he simply enjoyed passing his fingers over cracked surfaces and observing the many, intricate ways an object can crack and break. Perhaps he had even broken the object himself, anew, again and again, just for the pleasure of seeing the hundreds and thousands of pieces fall apart before picking them up and piecing them back together again.

Later on during her stay with him, he shared his secrets with her. He initiated her to his craft's intricacies, its redundancies, its frustrations and to its final, broken beauty. But this unnamed apprenticeship had sunk to the back of her mind like a falling star shooting through the darkness and the emptiness, to reappear when Aya began to recognize Abensour Stirling's presence in the way she crafted her art.

Abensour Stirling looked up and interpreted Aya's puzzled expression for one of admiration and longing. He chuckled.

"There is some of my father's artistic genius in me, isn't there? I too make up and tell my own stories, through these ancient, broken objects."

She wanted to reply, "All that you are saying, over and over again, is that your father, the great James Stirling, the man who didn't even leave you with a portrait to hold, is indeed your father." But she didn't, for his world of sophisticated half-truths was new to her, and Abensour Stirling was as opaque as a shattered mirror.

He went on: "And it's in you, too. Sometimes talent passes from one being to the next in mysterious ways, does it not?"

But it was important that she stay focused on the reason she had come to see him.

"Mr. Abensour, I would like to pay a visit to my family."

Abensour Stirling stared quietly at her, his brow stern, as though gauging how best to answer her request. A smile spread slowly across his face. She watched him, holding her breath. Despite the smile and Abensour Stirling's obvious effort at kindliness, Aya sensed a pent-up aggressiveness, the latent residue of years of self-doubt and suspicion. She saw, in the depth of his eyes and the white of his teeth, a dog, barely restrained on a loose leash. She watched, heard a snap, thought she saw Abensour Stirling's inner dog break free of his hesitant grasp, lunge at her. It must have been in her head. An acute pain exploded there and spread through her body, down her back, her limbs, her palms to her fingertips, her ankles to her feet. This would be the first of many such spells. She swayed but didn't buckle.

He said to her: "You wish to see your family?"

"I do. My mother and father must be worried about me."

"Are they now?"

His eyes turned cold.

"Aya, you may not like what you find, if you go back there."

"I do not expect to find anything. I would like to see my family, that's all."

"Go. But do so at your own risk."

"I will never blame you for anything, Mr. Abensour Stirling. You have been kind."

He looked at Aya suspiciously, distrusting this meekness that was so unlike her. And he was right. It was not meekness. It was her recognition of his gift to her. It was a broken, uneven, unwanted gift, but she didn't underestimate its value. She had stepped into a closed, privileged world that didn't easily open up to outsiders, but whose advantages were incommensurate. For her, it was her way out of Tangiers. So, why did she not feel grateful or proud?

Abensour Stirling waved his hand at her: "Go then. But don't pretend I didn't warn you. Don't forget what I saved you from."

She nodded and left the room. Warn her of what? He had issued no warning, only barely veiled threats.

She stepped out of the cool, bougainvillea-covered neighborhood and picked her way carefully down the steep alleyways and stone-paved streets. The few weeks she had spent in the high hills of Tangiers had already transformed Aya's relationship with the city. Its once familiar streets and sidewalks had become barriers she must trudge through, hurdles she must overcome. It had become unfamiliar, foreign and strange. It was as if she had forgotten the city, or the city had forgotten her.

As she walked through the tortuous streets and into the poorer, traditional neighborhoods she grew up in, she felt uneasy, scared even. Nothing seemed right or in its place. Where once she had enjoyed its scents and noise, now she felt revulsion and disgust. The pungent scents hid beneath their sweetness the dirt and the overused cooking oil. The loud noises were not conversations, light exchanges or joyful banter; they were the harsh, desperate attempts at selling wares no one wanted.

Aya felt out of place in her old neighborhood. The air rang, hostile to her. Once friendly neighbors shot quick, uneasy glances in her direction, others turned away or spat on the ground, in front of her.

She walked as fast as she could, her sneakers hitting the pavement in soft thuds. As she approached her family's apartment, in the rundown building at the end of the street, she turned cold. She stopped in front of the main door. The building's façade was blackened and looked deserted.

She looked up toward the third floor, toward the window of her parents' apartment. It too was blackened, the glass of the windowpane shattered and the curtains torn. She leaned back, tried to look inside. It seemed empty. She hesitated, then walked toward the main door. She placed her hand on the doorknob. It was covered in an ashen dust. She looked at her palm, at her fingers, at the strange map traced by the ashes on her skin. Complicated, muffled thoughts raced through her head. A man walked up to her and his shadow covered the sidewalk.

"They're gone."

Aya turned to face him.

"Who's gone?"

"Your family. They're gone."

"What happened here?"

"Don't you remember?"

"What should I remember?"

"Nobody told you?"

"Told me what?"

"That man who came for you...He knows what happened."

Aya stared at the building.

"There was a fire. It came from the apartment, and spread."

"When?"

"The day you left. November twenty-seventh."

"How did the fire start?"

But instinctively Aya knew, as though it could never have been otherwise. From the day Kareem turned off the light in the bedroom on him and her. From the day his black, burning eyes turned to ash and his dreams to cinder.

Aya began to shiver uncontrollably. A fire could warm her now. The man shielded his eyes from the glare of the sun. She said to him:

"Why didn't they come for me?"

"Oh child, how could they? Don't you understand?"

"My brother, Kareem?"

"The boy. They came for him."

"Is he alive?"

The man lowered his head.

"They say he is, the only one to have survived."

His words punctured the air, and Aya was filled with white-hot rage.

"And my mother and father? Answer me. I have a right to know."

"They're gone, child. Your brother survived because he wasn't there when the fire started…Didn't anyone tell you?"

"Is he the reason the fire started?"

"Who am I to judge what I haven't seen."

"Where is he?"

"They came for him, the police, the authorities. But he had disappeared. We never saw him again."

"He's still alive?"

"Maybe. Now go, go back to that man who came for you. Forget all that you saw. It's already forgotten by everyone else."

"What do you mean, gone? Tell me: are my mother and father alive?" Aya asked again.

But the man had already turned his back and disappeared down the alleyway at the end of the street.

———

Aya stood in front of the blackened façade, for how long she couldn't tell. The sun had gone down. The *muezzin* had sung his prayer, and the streets had turned a golden brown. She held her head up, pulled her hair back, filled with a certainty that could not, and should not, speak itself.

She would never know what happened to her family, but she knew she would never see them again. Rumors about them abounded for a while, before thinning out and finally disappearing. Aya even heard that they had escaped the fire and left the city. But those were witches' tales, for people her parents' age rarely left anymore, and the man had said they didn't survive.

It was also said that Kareem had stood outside his burning home until the police came for him. That he had attacked a policeman and cut through his abdomen with a long knife, as payment for the pain the guard had inflicted on his mother one perfect day, at a princely beach.

Or, that he had gone to fight the jihad in Afghanistan. Or that he had embarked on a wooden boat that may, or may not, have made it to the other side—Spain, Italy, Norway.

But being on the lookout for information, believing hearsay, was a dangerous enterprise. Aya would quickly learn to close her eyes and ears to the world.

She wandered the city for days before ringing Abensour Stirling's doorbell.

thirty-one

After what seemed to her a very long time, the front door opened and she was allowed in. Was the humiliating wait his way of reminding her of how lucky she was to be a part of his household?

She found Abensour Stirling sitting at his long, cracked, blackened dining table. The veneer of precious sophistication had worn itself out, and the house's carcass—or Abensour Stirling's soul—emerged.

Abensour Stirling sat, surrounded by peeled purple grapes and a silver coffee service. He held a cup of coffee in one hand and spat out grape stones into the palm of his other hand, without looking up.

"Did you ever wonder why they never came to see you?"

"I thought it was because you had asked them not to," she replied.

"No. They're gone."

"There was a fire."

"Yes. Who told you?"

"A neighbor, and a crumbling façade."

"An accident?"

"Kareem killed them."

"Ah, you don't know this…No one knows this."

"Someone started that fire. Who else could it be?"

"An accident. Proof?"

"Their disappearance."

"How do you know Kareem also died?"

"He may not have died. But he has vanished. They're all gone."

The sound of the fruit being spit into his palm bore into Aya's nerves. She wanted the noise to stop. But Abensour Stirling was not about to stop. He looked at her, as his rounded mouth spat the stones into his white palms.

Aya stared back. This surprised him, as he was not used to open defiance.

She didn't protest. She didn't run or complain. She just stood still, facing him. What he did not see were her clenched fists and teeth. After all, how could he have known that every experience in her life had taught her how to stuff the unbearable into little boxes and close them forever.

He sat back, deep in thought. There was admiration, even some kindness, in his gesture when he pointed to a chair at his side.

"Come, sit. Have some coffee and grapes. The coffee is hot and the grapes are sweet."

Aya sat where he pointed. Her limbs felt stiff and brittle. She felt a sudden, strange pity for this man, orphaned of family and country, who, without conviction, had taken on a ward. She drank the hot, bitter coffee and bit into the grapes' overly sweet flesh.

———

If Aya's experiences in Abensour Stirling's household could be strung together, each experience set within another like Russian dolls, she would have to conclude that he had been more kind than cruel.

He had kept his promises—some of them. He had helped her up when others had abandoned her, shown her places that others could not. He had picked up where Miss Mai could carry her no further, where her parents had given up. He had also showed her a hole in the wall, told her of an elsewhere beyond Tangiers, out of Africa. While her wildest dreams never took her further than the European coastline she could see from her window, huddled in a small wooden *patera*, he promised her other crossings, other destinations, ones more gentle and humane. He promised papers, legitimacy, an education at one of the American universities the world revolved around. For Abensour Stirling had his ways and connections, which he used to help Aya.

Living with Abensour Stirling had forced her to break from her flat, linear view of the world, and her insignificant place in it. He had given her a chance to discover a rounded world of choice and privilege, and to find her own route through it. This was Abensour Stirling's ultimate gift to her, one that she recognized beyond the guilt at being chosen while others were not. At being one of those select few who had the divine good fortune to cross over on a plane, papers in hand, and not at sea, in wooden boats sunken by the weight of their human cargo.

There were other ways to get out of Tangiers, and its dead ends. But for all her grit and talent, Aya would probably never have found her way out, had it not been for pure luck—in the person of Abensour Stirling.

And so Aya followed him, from a painful, shameful experience to a most extraordinary and strange conclusion: She agreed to close her eyes and let her mind wander when, at night, he would lean toward her and say,

"Forget where you are from. Forget, or the memories

will bring you down with them. Forget…"

And though he never touched her in the way that Kareem had, the eerie, cruel words that Abensour Stirling whispered to her at night haunted her dreams and filled her with fear.

Aya would forget. She even forgot that day, when, walking down a busy Tangiers boulevard, she thought she saw them, all three of them—her mother, father and Kareem—on the other side of the street, a peaceful, tightly knit family. She also forgot that she crossed to the other side of the street, only to find that they were already gone, hurrying down the bustling street, lost among a sea of strangers.

thirty-two

Aya lay on her back on the floor. She shook all over, her body drenched in sweat. Her memories swirled in front of her. They rose and blended into the ceiling above, vague images, residues of colors, fragments, broken and brittle like thin ice. She couldn't understand how these memories had come back to her, after a thousand and one years of absence, of emptiness and rootlessness.

It all had started, she realized, the day she heard the blind pianist play. David always pretended he didn't hear him. That there was no one there and no musician ever played on his floor.

That day she heard the pianist play, an uncontrollable sadness took hold of Aya, one that gave way to anguish. Not long after, the first memory emerged. Clear and delicate, slow, careful, it arrived like a stranger hesitant to intrude but in need of a place to stay for the night. It spoke in a soft, gentle voice, almost tender.

Gradually, it brought forth other memories: longer, stronger, more complex. They came in the aspect of colors and scenes. They even had their own voice, the voice that replaced her own, that became her when she remembered the past, when she put the past to paper and wrote through its eyes. It was a powerful voice—needy, greedy. It wanted to linger by her side, invade her space, colonize her thoughts, steal ever longer breaks in time. It wanted to take over.

This voice rang in her ears and wiped out any resistance to it. The images it called forth grew increasingly bright and strong. And she couldn't tell if they were real or fabricated. Lying on the hard floor, she wondered whose voice it was. What did it want from her? Where was it taking her?

———————

Aya stood and faced the canvas. She needed to finish the painting by evening. Ari would be there soon. She couldn't quit so close to the finish line.

She began to paint. She painted furiously, like a soldier trying to cover a fatal mistake, like a magician trying to re-call forces he had unleashed and that had escaped him. She painted to reverse time, to fix what was broken. To forget what had been irretrievably lost.

As Aya worked, the canvas rose toward her, eager to talk to her. She wanted to toss her brush aside and plunge her hands inside the canvas to retrieve its essence. The deep, thick, warm, living essence that she knew was inside, that had been stolen from her.

Beads of sweat trickled down her forehead, cooling her. The ringing in her ears was deafening. She knew she couldn't continue for much longer. But something was missing from the painting. It seemed to be keeping its secret from her. She looked closely at it. Did it not want to be completed?

Her phone rang. The ringtones were *talking* to her: reminding her of a task left undone, a person forgotten, a porcelain rose, a black wall, stone grapes.

She picked up her phone and saw that someone had left

a message, the same message that had plagued her for years without fail. But this year, and for the first time, it was sent to her twice, within weeks. And twice it came with the added line. Three lines, four words each, and now the added four words in the final line. A nonsensical line, hanging loosely at the end of a closed message. Aya read the lines, written in the Spanish of her Tangiers childhood.

> *A medida que el fuego arde.*
> *El viaje se convierte en pérdida*
> *La partida al exilio*
> *Y la muñeca se rompe.*

She tried to delete the message, but the words stayed on the screen. She kept trying, but the message was undeletable. For the first time in all those years, she read the message aloud.

At first, the Spanish words were difficult to pronounce. Her tongue tripped on the words of her mother tongue, the language her mother and grandmother used in tenderness, in rituals of love and remembrance, mixed in with the singsong Arabic of Tangiers, when speaking to a child, or to one's beloved. A language Aya had forgotten she knew, one that she had buried beneath French and English, and that she believed she'd left behind, oceans and continents away. What did these words mean? Why did they come to her twice, and why the added word, twice?

As she looked at the words, they blurred into color—vibrant, intense, liquid blues, greens and reds.

> *As the fire burns*
> *The journey becomes loss*
> *The departure exile*
> *And the muñeca breaks.*

Muñeca...Doll. Two words that tried to conjure the same thing, but that instead could only offer imperfect mirrors of one another. Brittle words, made of porcelain and of stiff, useless material, like the muñeca-doll itself, the two languages imagined to be one and the same.

Aya's eyes glazed and rolled upward. Blinding color gave way to alternating blackness and whiteness, a macabre dance of dark and light. When it stopped, she saw, in the background, a woman in a painting gesturing to her with her ringed hands to come closer. She approached her and saw that she was two: two women, holding hands—one in European dress, the other in indigenous Mexican dress.

As Aya came closer, she saw that the European dress was tinged with the indigenous, and the indigenous dress was tinged with the European. Their hearts were not the same: they had two hearts, and one fed from the other, weakening it. And she could sense, with relief, their physical suffering, the relentless ache of their shattered body.

They smiled at her, opened their arms and whispered to her: They were two. They had always been two, never one. And that was the only way it could be. They reached out their jeweled hands and necks to her, drawing her to them, as though to invite her into their private dance, their shared secret.

She held her breath, extending her fingers toward them, eager to touch their bright colors. But when Aya's hands met theirs, they turned into porcelain, cold and hard, their bodies and faces, a thin, ashen white. And when she tried to hold on to them, to find comfort in their presence, they shattered into hundreds of pieces at her feet.

———

Aya stood in the middle of her studio, her phone sitting lightly in her hands. The glaze had cleared and she could see again.

She remembered the doll she had, which she had loved very much, when she was a little girl. Her father had driven to Sebta, a Spanish enclave on Moroccan territory east of Tangiers, and had brought it back for her. It was just before the Spanish government made it hard for citizens of Tangiers to enter the Spanish enclaves on Moroccan soil. So her father, like many of his friends, would drive once a year to Sebta to buy necessities they couldn't acquire in Tangiers: clothes, towels, kitchen appliances, household items. Aya's family was far from rich, and his yearly trip to Sebta helped them manage their expenses.

One year, when she was five, her father bought her a Spanish porcelain doll, a muñeca from the legendary Marin factory in Andalusia. She was beautiful, dressed in a traditional red-and-black flamenco dress, with high heels, and hair tied in a bun, held by a golden *peineta* comb. Her cheeks and her lips were red, and her body was frozen in a flamenco dance move: rigid, graceful, unchanging.

The Marin muñeca slept in Aya's bed and stayed with her, until the day Kareem took it away from her. Though she had the doll for over a decade, she never paid particular attention to it. Aya wasn't like other children, attached to a particular toy, caressing it like a pet or speaking to it like a secret friend. The Marin muñeca was just there, and Aya liked her limpness, her unruffled dress and gleaming hair. Yet, a doll was an insignificance, a passing incandescence in a childhood no longer remembered or cherished by anyone, ordinary, unquestioned, unappreciated.

Aya tried to remember more, but the heavy fog wouldn't

lift. Was there something important she needed to remember? She fought to find the answers. She vaguely remembered that, though the doll never left her bed, though she held its delicate porcelain hand and believed she could even hear its heart beat, she didn't cherish it. In fact, Aya was scared of it. She felt tied to it as though its presence in her room, on her bed, was obligatory, and that it was there to watch her.

The muñeca was the only present her father ever gave her. He was a frugal man who didn't believe in toys or gifts. He never spent on any gadgets for himself, and he was even stricter with Aya than with Kareem. And yet, when she received it from his hands, she felt neither joy nor pride. She felt that she was now tied to the muñeca, indebted to it for her father's sake. She felt pressed to become the little girl the father thought her to be: delicate, made of porcelain, fragile, sweet, perfectly balanced in an eternal, frozen, graceful, traditional dance.

When Abensour Stirling came for Aya, when she tried to take the doll with her and Kareem took it away, she was relieved. Something broke, but it was a good thing. She was not a little girl anymore and the thoughts that stumbled in her head and nagged her day and night, also began to break down. Something was wrong with Aya. She didn't know what it was, when it started or when it—*she*—broke. But here it was, and here she was.

The muñeca *had* to be the key to finishing the painting. It rested in her hands, as a word on a flashing screen, once again. Who could have sent it? Was it a guardian angel, an evil spirit, or the American agents, disguised as normal citizens, that had been watching her ever since she'd arrived on their shores?

Then she realized that the painting wanted to be more

than just a painting. Despite her best efforts at making them rise, the colors of the oil paints remained soft, flat, linear, for they craved to transform into matter. She had to feed it something else.

thirty-three

Aya stepped out of her studio, through the glass doors and into her apartment. In the kitchen, she took out the Moroccan tea glasses and wrapped them in a towel. Then she crushed them beneath her feet.

The broken pieces were small and they shimmered. She touched them gently with her fingertips, and the pieces scratched at her. She let drops of blood drip onto the broken glass and watched as their surfaces became tainted red. The glass looked like a blood-red flower.

She picked up the broken pieces, wet and shining, and, carrying them in her arms, walked back through the glass doors and into the studio. She had to pause to open the doors, wide open only a minute ago. She didn't recall having closed them.

Aya stood in front of the painting, holding the broken shards of the Moroccan tea glasses. The glasses may or may not have belonged to Abensour Stirling's mother, or may or may not have been purchased by Aya in an antique shop in Cambridge that offered wares from around the world, sold as ancient and valuable for the simple reason that they were foreign. Aya couldn't clearly recall how she came to own the set of slender glasses.

She stood in front of the painting, holding the shards of glass in her arms like an offering to a vengeful deity. The last stretch was always the most difficult, the one where she was the most plagued by self-doubt.

She picked out pieces of glass and placed them on the canvas. She worked for hours, for each piece seemed to have a single purpose, a single place inside the painting. The pieces gleamed, red and filled with light, on the canvas. At first, they appeared to be placed at random, and she herself didn't know if it was a catalytic force that moved them, or recklessness that moved her.

Some pieces sank to the bottom of the painting, while others lingered at its surface, held in place by the sticky, half-dried paint. Soon, all the pieces had been placed. Finally, she painted in her signature slanted, blood red, aleph-like flower at the bottom of the canvas. Aya breathed slowly as the last rays of the sun sank behind the skyscrapers lining the horizon…

It was done.

She had finished just in time. Ari would come for it tonight, or tomorrow morning. Perhaps he would allow her one extra night with the painting before taking it away.

Aya stepped back, lowered her eyes to her paint-stained hands and finally found the courage to look.

There it was.

She expected to feel some sense of achievement. Instead, she felt nothing. She just stood there, quietly, while her solitude bore down on her. She couldn't hear a sound or feel a thing.

Aya stared at the painting, trying to understand it. She touched the canvas, gently, so as not to disturb the wet paint and settling matter. She couldn't describe it. It was as though she were expected to understand an unknown, foreign language. To her surprise, its surface was warm and soft. Yet, there was no similarity between the way it felt and the way it looked.

Aya leaned her head toward the painting, closed her eyes and smelled it. It smelled of peat and brine. Driven by a peculiar instinct, she stuck out her tongue and licked the surface, close to the corner. It tasted like…dust, or ashes. She then put her ear close to it, and she could hear the sound of waves crashing on a tall, black, impregnable cliff. She put her ear even closer to the canvas and heard a voice snickering at her behind the waves, wind and thunder. It was a metallic voice, one born in anger and bred on steel and fire. It grated:

"Unloved Aya Dane, dispossessed Aya Dane, unneeded Aya Dane, you should have drowned at sea with the others, the foul, the wretched, the weak of the earth."

An acute pain, which she thought was a lightning strike from the storm hiding behind the painting, tore through her and left her breathless.

She stepped back and looked at it again. Something was there, something she hadn't noticed before. The broken shards of glass scattered across the canvas formed a shape. It was a doll: a limp, discarded doll, with a torn red dress, extending into the depths of the painting. Even there, inside an artwork, she found the doll insignificant and ordinary. Though its unwanted presence in her painting terrified her, its banality soothed her fear into a dull, inconsequential anger.

Why was it there? Aya suspected that it had summoned itself to deny her right to forget it, her right to not care about it and what had happened to it. Perhaps it was even looking for what was left of Aya's childhood, to take that away from her. It was there to torture her. It wanted to destroy her.

After all these years, Aya felt grateful toward Abensour Stirling. He had freed her from the doll, from the overbearing nostalgia of a childhood inside a family that had turned its back on her. He had helped her forget about love and tenderness. He had taught her to accept that love was not for her, and that human warmth and kindness would always be denied her. He had showed her the hard way, the difficult way, that she had to fend for herself.

Now, with the doll's fixed presence in her final work, Aya could no longer contain her unwanted solitude. It exploded and was mirrored in the painting. In fact, it was clear to her that the muñeca had been in the painting the entire time, from the first touch of the brush on canvas. It filled the canvas with the anxiety and uncertainty that she herself had succumbed to when she began painting it.

The finished work had become her own, intimate enemy.

thirty-four

The colors in the painting reached out and surrounded Aya with their presence. The flamenco dress twirled and widened to hide the sunlight and darken the room. Aya realized then that she couldn't give the painting to Ari.

To pick up the broken pieces of her past and breathe life into them…Perhaps that had been her struggle ever since she first put brush to paint to canvas.

The voice in her head, it was also inside the painting. She could hear it, grating, scratching to get out, multiplying, eager to spill the images it carried within itself. They were everywhere, they always had been, but they had remained hidden, till now. They were the exile she carried within. The lingering remnants, the rituals, the intricate details. They were the reason she couldn't find and share the love of another person.

She had thought she could survive the crossing, could bury the homeland. She'd thought she would survive in this new world, in Boston. But to survive in America, one must first get rid of nostalgia, put the haunting memories in a cupboard along with the dusty tea glasses, probably bought in a farmers' market by the Charles River. Bury past, land, family, before seeing them bloom again at a single touch of light after decades of darkness. Her unfathomable illness had caught up with her at last.

But she didn't know if the memories were real. Were they another trap, and if they were, who was out to get her, who wanted to destroy her? Who sent her the messages and what did they know of the fire that burned down her home?

The answer must be contained in her painting, in the voice inside it. It resounded like the echo of echoes, and she was certain that it held the key to her brokenness. This, her signature work, *was* Aya: it was strange like her. She couldn't give it away, she couldn't be split in such a way, beyond repair. But she couldn't keep it, either.

There was only one choice: She had to burn the painting before Ari came for it. It too had to burn, like her family.

As this idea took shape, the doorbell rang. It was too late. Aya knew who was standing outside the front door. The wilderness that had taken hold of her over the last hours subsided, and she was left with the inevitability of what was to come. The doorbell rang again, louder.

thirty-five

Aya pushed the painting into a dark corner of the studio, between the used paints and yellowed sketches, making sure it was well hidden. She went downstairs and opened the door.

She found a nondescript, ageless man standing there. The appearance of the man in front of her had no particular identifying sign. It provided no hints as to his personality, origins or age. There was something anonymous and banal about him, a vapidity that was disturbing. He could have been from the Transvaal, the Gujarat or the island of Corsica. Every country in the world could claim him as one of theirs. He was the type of person who, if he were to walk down a street, people would perhaps glance at, but then immediately forget.

He never introduced himself as Ari, nor did he say a word of greeting to her. But Aya knew it was him. He had come at the end of the last day, as promised, arriving when the sun begins to set behind the horizon and when the city begins to go quiet for the long night ahead.

She braced at the anxiety of the coming interaction. The Malian street musician was her next-to-last encounter with a fellow human being, and he had left a lingering melody in his wake that shielded her from the roughness of the world. Kareem was her last encounter, and he had exploded that melody and opened her up, once more, to the cruelty of the world lying in wait.

Here, then, was Ari.

He shot a quick glance at Aya. He seemed annoyed. He then looked beyond her, as though her presence were a nuisance. She sensed his repulsion and noticed a hunger in his eyes, as he looked past her. He was not in the least curious about or interested in her. His shoulder scraped against hers and she stepped back.

Once inside, his agitation increased. He spoke in a low, soft voice, and she couldn't detect the origins of his accent's peculiar inflections. It could have been Eastern European, Latin or even Middle Eastern. It was like no accent she had ever heard. He had the accent of things that are cut out and forgotten: the piece of land flooded to create the Panama Canal, for instance, or the trees felled to build the boats carrying refugees across oceans. He turned to find Aya staring at him.

"Where is it?" he asked.

Her thoughts turned briefly to the dark, dusty corner where she had hidden her painting. Immediately, he hurried across the floor, through the glass doors and into the studio. His eyes swept intently across the walls and floors. He sniffed the air like a wolf, searching for prey in the barren steppes.

"Where is it?" he asked again, his tone sharp.

Aya froze at the harshness in his voice. Beads of sweat trickled down her back, and an acute pain wracked her head and neck.

"We had an understanding. I've come a long way."

Aya was filled with desire. It was an ancient desire—the palpable incarnation of ambition, of power, the desire to be known, to leave a mark on the world. A desire that defied death, and time itself. It was an elemental craving for recognition, for which she had agreed to be taken to the brink. She thought of David, and the love and life she might have had with him. But she also remembered how his intentions toward her were always unclear, and that she could never quite pinpoint or understand them. What she did know was that love could be a drug, a medication to stun and numb. Love was a mental illness for women like her. It could swerve them from the rightful path. For, wasn't love—beyond the warmth of an embrace, beyond the tenderness of mingled breath or beyond the children she would never have—a prison, a violence, in truth the greatest of lies?

Silently, Aya glanced toward the shadows where the old paints and the sketches played in the dust and shone softly in the red light of the dying day. Ari, his touch cold and wet, pushed past her and walked directly to the painting. With his back to her, he stood in front of the canvas, picked it up and held it carefully to the light. Slowly then, he walked to the middle of the studio, to the exact spot where she had painted the piece, and where the lighting was best. There he set down the canvas in front of him.

She thought that his slumped back expressed disappointment in the work he had been so eager to see. She called him by his name, but he neither answered nor moved. Perhaps he hadn't heard her?

Aya took a deep breath, walked up to him and stood next to him in front of the canvas. She tried to see what he saw: the shards of glass, the colors, both opaque and delicate, rough and subdued. She stood frozen in place, for she realized she had given him her debris, her brokenness. She tried to breathe, but her chest burned and even the intake of air hurt as she watched him.

Ari was staring at the painting, completely still, his face expressionless. His back was limp, his legs and arms stiff. Nothing in him seemed alive, except for his hands, which were clenching and unclenching uncontrollably. He turned to her, his face pale, his expression glazed.

Slowly, Aya understood. She looked at the painting again to see what he saw, to reimagine it anew, through his eyes. His hands had relaxed, and the studio was filled with his silence. It was a calm, restful silence that carried within it the expectations of dreams come true. Whose dreams? It was a light, feathery silence like none she had ever experienced before; the graceful silence that precedes dawn and the playful silence of an awakening after a centennial sleep.

A smile appeared on her lips. Though she still couldn't wrap her head around what was happening, the conclusion was evident: she had succeeded. Ari had accepted her painting. In fact, he craved and desired it. It was a rare hunger, one that could only be satiated by the full possession of what he had seen. A rush of unprecedented pride coursed through Aya, and she felt invincible. She momentarily forgot her tortured mind and her wilted body. They didn't matter anymore.

Ari's voice interrupted her thoughts.

"It must be taken away from here, protected..."

He continued mumbling and cursing to himself as he rummaged through the studio, looking behind easels and bottles of paint and turpentine. Finally, he found what he was looking for. He dragged two cardboard boxes into the middle of the room, flattened them out, set the painting on the first, and covered it with the second, leaving a space between the cardboard and the painting. He picked it up and cradled it in his arms. In a moment, Ari and the painting would be out of Aya's life for good.

Could she truly let it go? Was that what the painting demanded of her?

An image of her brother lying on the ground flashed before her eyes. His blood, a red flower on the white snow, a gun in his closed hand. The image dissipated, and there was Ari, hurrying to the door, without even a glance in her direction.

"Wait. Not yet," she called out to him, her voice cold and mechanical.

Ari turned to her in surprise, as though he had forgotten that she was there. Again, he looked at her with distaste.

"Wait," Aya called out again, her words heavy stones in her mouth. "Where are you taking my painting?"

"I'm accepting the painting," he replied matter-of-factly. "You will never see it again."

He took out a piece of paper from a briefcase, which she hadn't noticed when he walked in. The piece of paper was a contract in which she, Aya Dane, agreed to sell Ari her painting for one million gold crowns.

"Once you sign this contract, the gold crowns will be wired to your account. In return, you agree to never look for your painting, or its holding place, for as long as you live. That's all you need to do. If you don't respect this part of the contract, your work will be destroyed and you will disappear, as though the earth had never held you."

He handed her a pen. She hesitated, her desire as deep as his hunger was wide.

"I haven't even had a chance to name it yet."

"I name it. It's mine. I choose. I create. I call the painting by the name of the artist it is my good will to acquire. This one will be known as the *Aya Dane*."

"Will anyone ever see it?"

"The world doesn't deserve its masterworks. It doesn't understand them. It condemns them, denigrates them, and when it does recognize their true value, it sells them to undeserving fools, eager to promote their own ambitions."

Aya's head ached. She looked for breath and words.

He took out a cigarette and lit it. A puff of yellow smoke surrounded him in a filmy haze. Sheets of glass seemed to appear from nowhere and to create a block around him and the painting. It was as if his power had no limit. The pain in Aya's head became unbearable waves of loss.

His personhood was a denial of presence, of exile and loss. He was of nowhere and everywhere. He existed without awareness of the emptiness brought about by severed roots, denial, forgetfulness, erasure.

Or were these, once again, the ravings of an inflamed mind?

An image of David then flashed before her, and she imagined a legion of enemies crouched behind him, waiting for any sign of weakness. She inhaled burning air: she had been right, in the end, to get rid of love, which was only ever betrayal.

"Will you take care of my painting?"

"It will join my collection. It will become a legend."

"Where is it, your collection?"

Ari became cautious. His harsh tone softened.

"In the most beautiful place in the world. Where your painting will always be safe."

She took the pen from his outstretched hand, and signed.

The smoke and glass that seemed to surround him disappeared as though they had never been there. The ache in her head subsided, and the air cleared.

He picked up the painting, stepped across the threshold separating the apartment from the studio, went downstairs and left. From the doorway, she watched him stride away from the house and into the darkness. She thought she heard her Malian friend's music follow him through the quiet streets, a melody of crystalline lightness that carried her forgotten desires in its folds.

Ari had left as he had come: without sound or emotion, shrouded in vagueness and a deep, unsettling banality. He'd left as if he had never set foot there in the first place, as if he were a figment of her imagination.

———

Aya went upstairs and stared at her reflection in the glass panels of her studio door. She ran her hands over her shaved head and noted how nondescript her own face looked. Even the color of her eyes had faded, their light subdued and ash-ridden. What had she done?

The vibrant flashes of color in the painting were flashes of her own color, flashes of *her*. They didn't belong to it, they belonged to her, they were of her.

What, exactly, had she given away? A terrible suspicion swept over her. She searched inside her heart for that desire, that hunger to paint, that urge to touch color and put form to canvas; that obsessive creativity that had crouched behind her every thought, memory, action. But she found only emptiness and lack.

The inner sense of color, shape and form, was gone. The ebullience and fire were gone. Her dread and doubt grew.

She dragged an easel to the light, placed a canvas in its triangle and took out her paints. She cleaned a brush in turpentine and water, and put its tip to the canvas. The canvas shrieked and the paints ran, weak and thin, on her fingers. She began to draw. The brush felt clumsy between her fingers, and when she looked at what she had drawn, she saw ragged lines and strange scribbles. She tried again and again, her face and body drenched in sweat. And each time, she ended up with the same result: lines, unending and meaningless, and peculiar symbols. She put down her paints and brushes; she could no longer paint.

At that moment, she understood. Ari was not after a painting. He had come for *her*. Along with his commissioned work, he had taken her memories, her foreignness, her Arabness, her nothingness, her talents, her dreams, her loves…her soul. Until now, she'd forgotten that she even had one. She thought she had left it behind, somewhere in Tangiers, with the family that had abandoned her, the neighborhood that had forgotten her, the home that had burnt down, inside the cold house of Abensour Stirling.

Aya had become a poor copy of Frida Kahlo, without the strong and weak hearts and the joined hands. She had become a caricature, an embarrassment. She was nothing more than an impostor and a fraud.

In the moment when she gave away the painting that held her name, the veil lifted and she was left with nothing. He had taken it all with him, and she had let him.

Ari, her own intimate, original and final, madness.

———

Aya locked herself up in the studio. She slipped in and out of consciousness, unable to tell the difference between the real and the imaginary, the clear truth and imagined memories, and between day and night.

After what could have been hours or days, months or years, she was able to get up, take a shower and prepare herself a small meal. Black coffee and burnt toast. The hot coffee coursed through her and energized her. The burnt toast gave her strength. She looked at herself in the mirror. Her body was bone thin and stooped, emptied of itself. Far away were her days of black outfits and flowery scarves. Her body could no longer wear anything with grace or style. Where had Aya Dane gone?

thirty-six

Aya sat at the table, staring at the sheets of paper in the lined notebook that she couldn't remember having written, but knew were hers. In the margins were smudges of ink, red like plastered roses. She pressed her pen against the paper and picked up where she'd left off sometime earlier, though she didn't know when.

All she still knew was that these pages were for you, the stranger in her home, the persecutor in the armchair—every event she believed to have happened, starting from the day she received Ari's letter, the day she'd heard the music of a blind pianist who had come to her through the mist forming around and inside her. In his gentle, broken notes were cradled all those who had, with such casual cruelty, danced her to the end of love.

What remained was doubt, and with it, the unspeakable fear that her memories, and the voices that whispered of them, had failed her or, worse, had tricked her, *lied* to her...

Colors, fragments from her life in Tangiers flooded her. Now they seemed an intricate bundle of lies, fabricated to deceive her into believing that everything she now did—or thought of doing—was wrong.

She remembered a meeting with her brother Kareem, which had taken place not long ago on the icy bridge of a frozen river. But she couldn't tell for sure if it had happened. The pain in her head and body became excruciating.

She couldn't deny having once had a family, or that they had disappeared, that they had perished: in a fire, at sea, at the hands of the police, or of Kareem, or perhaps of sadness, joylessness, regret—the manner of their death was incidental. What mattered was that their love, too, had died.

Though her mother had promised to come with her to the deepest, darkest depths, she had left Aya there, alone. She had lost her father, to the weakness and shame that consumed him for not protecting his family, and she had lost her brother to the religiosity of rough men, to the hardness of a failed city. She had reached this place, America, only to lose herself in David's gaze, in his unclear love and self-interest.

The piercing pain that she now almost expected shot through her spine, neck and head, immobilizing her and cutting her stream of thoughts short.

She had been reading, writing, painting her own story wrong.

Aya once dreamt of happiness with David, in Boston. Fleetingly, she had even believed in peace. But she had never loved David. He was an illusion, a wronged, wrongful wish. She only wanted to believe that she had loved him.

Who had Aya loved, ever since she'd reached this country? Who had touched her heart, and she theirs?

Only Beck Vandeer and Ali Farka Touré, though she met them only in passing, and both were now gone. She had loved them, because, like her, they inhabited the outskirts. She'd loved them the only way she knew how, at the edge of her mind, the edge of her being, and in silence. Though her connection with them may have appeared weak and transient, it carried within it a dream of healing, kindness, hope, utopia.

Aya paused and put down her pen. She looked up at the room around her. Something was not quite right.

thirty-seven

She rose. The room around her blurred and shifted, rear-ranged itself and reappeared to her. The space—her space—was now a senseless space. It was as she knew it to be, and yet it was different.

Her leg hit a hard surface, and she turned. An old, dusty piano stood in the corner of the room. Had it always been there? She raised the lid and found pages of sheet music. They appeared new but were slightly bent at the edges from use. They'd recently been read, and probably played—"Dance Me to the End of Love." She stared at the sheet music, then looked around again, as if for the first time.

The fireplace was cold and didn't appear to have been used in ages. The walls were a bland, neutral white, and the kitchen beyond was small and bare. Could it still shelter a bronze tray, a silver teapot and colorful glasses from across the sea? She remembered the day she got the tea glasses, at that hole in the wall in the Medina of Tangiers, where the artisan shaped his bronze and silver wares. She hesitated, the memory quickly fading. Did she? Was that indeed where she had acquired those glasses?

She gazed at the far side of the room, but there were no glass doors leading into a studio. Instead, under the room's single window, she saw an easel, strewn canvases, used paints, and oils and paintbrushes lining the corners of the room. On the other side, by an unfinished painting, was a bed, her bed. The covers had fallen to the floor, their corners stiff from the spilled paint—blues, yellows, ochers.

She went over to the narrow window through which the light shone furiously into the room, leaning against the sill for support. She peered outside, her hands pressed against the cold glass panes, at the soft tumble of snow on the ground. Curving street lamps lit the road all the way to the river, lined by high poplars and oaks.

A siren sounded from below, like the one that used to break her school day, or her father's workday. She, who always withdrew from any noise or interruption, was drawn to this sound.

She opened the door and walked out of the room, her torn, graying scarf trailing behind her like a forgotten veil. She found herself in a large, dark hallway, its walls inlaid with wood paneling, leading to a regal Victorian staircase. There were other doors on either side of the hallway—the children's rooms, or were they guest rooms? Had there always been so many rooms in this house? The floor beneath her feet was cold: she stared down. It was linoleum. Despite its gilded appearance, she sensed that this place wasn't what it seemed.

At the end of the hallway, another door, and a light beneath it. She walked toward it, her feet silent on the cold floor. The doorknob twisted open.

She sank back into a corner, hidden from view. A man, his silhouette familiar, opened the door, closed it behind him and hurried down the hallway.

As she shuffled back in surprise, her feet made a high-pitched squeak on the shiny linoleum floor.

The man paused, turned and saw her figure huddled in the corner. He walked toward her. His features seemed blurred, his eyes, nose and mouth indistinct, like a wax figurine melting in the heat. His body vacillated in the darkness, lost its consistency, and she doubted whether it was truly him, but it had to be.

"Aya, did you want to see me?"

His voice was hollow and wisplike, stranded in moonlight.

"Wait inside," he said, pointing toward the door behind them. "It's always open for you. I'll be back in fifteen minutes."

Before she could answer, he'd gone, as though he'd never been there at all.

She walked toward the door leading into his office. She turned the doorknob, it opened easily, and she slipped inside.

———

Aya knew this room. She paused, fighting against the confusion clouding her mind.

She walked over to the mahogany desk in the middle of the room. Trembling, she opened the drawers—top, bottom, left and right—and slipped her hand beneath piles of papers, pushing aside files, unsure of what she was looking for but knowing instinctively that, whatever it was, she would find it there. Pushing her hand in further, she tapped the wood, feeling its hollowness.

She checked underneath the table. There was a garbage can filled to the brim with papers. She picked it up, poured its contents onto the table and raked through it. Then she swept the trash back into the can.

She hesitated, a suspicion filling her mind. She opened

the bottom drawer again, her fingers looked around once more. And there, in the back of the drawer, beneath torn and crumpled sheets of paper, she felt an object.

It was a small black device, a voice recorder. It appeared to have been damaged, dented in one corner, but it looked like it would still function. She slipped it into her pocket, stuffed the crumpled papers back into the drawer and hurried out of the office.

As she walked softly up the corridor back to her room, a voice stopped her.

"Aya, did you not want to see me?"

She spun around to face the man standing behind her, tall and fair-skinned, his eyes unreadable in the dim light.

"It's fine," she muttered. "It can wait."

"Get some rest. We'll talk tomorrow, then."

She nodded, retreated toward her room and closed the door behind her.

She tried to lock her door but realized that there were no locks on it. She waited, but he hadn't followed her. His footsteps receded into the distance.

She sat down at her table, took the recorder out of her pocket, and pressed play.

thirty-eight

... I've just finished listening to Aya Dane read again to me from her journal. I'd asked her to pin down her story, since the morning she supposedly received an invitation from an anonymous patron, as meticulously as possible. As though she were painting a detailed landscape. I told her it was part of her treatment.

I'd gotten the idea when I saw she could no longer paint and that her mental state was deteriorating rapidly. I thought her writing might help unlock her most terrifying memories.

I had no certainty it would work. I've tried alternative methods in the past, with mixed results. I'll never know their full impact on a patient's mind, which can never be fully understood, no matter what any doctor may claim.

But beyond her journal's use as a therapeutic tool, I also just wanted—needed—to know more about her. To enter the meanders of her mind, to touch what was beyond my reach. The softness that lay beneath ...

... I knew that crossing the lines with her would change me, as much, if not more than, she might be changed by me. But I had my reasons—and, now, a diagnosis. After many painstaking hypotheses and wrong turns, I have a diagnosis,

one that justifies the cracks in the method and the porosity of boundaries or moral obligations.

I have a tangible expression of my hours of work, of painstaking interpretation, and doubt. I have the medical myth that claims that everything has an origin, and therefore an explanation and a cure, and a hope that the patient can be made whole again.

These red lines I've crossed with Aya, I've crossed them before, at another time, with another patient. In Paris, twenty years ago. I was a medical student interning at Sainte Jeanne, known then, and now, for its experimental treatment and approaches to mental illness.

I've always been fascinated by the force of instincts, dreams, repressed feelings—the inner war a person wages against his or her nightmares. I was fascinated by the migrant condition as a diagnostic category, by the fear and sense of displacement caused by exile. My supervisors sent me a patient, a young woman. She too, like Aya, was of North African origin.

This patient was young and beautiful, with an aching fragility that could leave no one indifferent. She was younger than I was, but I felt close to her, and she trusted me. My faculty noticed the trust she placed in me before I did, and they suggested I try alternative methods to heal her, or to help get a clear diagnosis of her diffuse symptoms.

And I did. I helped my supervisors … And I helped myself. I justified my interference by choosing to believe it would help her, too. I'd sit with her for hours in the hospital garden where she liked to spend her afternoons. We became friends, perhaps for her, more than friends. I began to look forward to our conversations, to our meetings, and—which should have troubled me then—so did she. I wrote detailed reports to my faculty, and they congratulated me on the thoroughness of my work.

The end came abruptly. My supervisors decided that I'd gathered enough information and that she was diagnosable, if not curable. They told me to stop seeing her, to move on to other patients and duties. They told me that my ambition and daring would take me far, but to keep close watch on my own failings, my masculine drive. To liberate myself from these impulses, they suggested I express myself freely in a personal audio journal, one that I could keep or destroy, at will.

I left Paris a couple of months after that. I never tried to get in touch with the young woman I treated, but I heard that she'd asked for me, and looked for me. I later heard that her condition worsened, that she never healed.

It took a long time to accept that her grace and beauty, her whimsical frailty, were just something I wanted to see—a partial image, my own projection and fantasy. And, in truth, what I refused to see was just how deeply troubled, scared and alone she was, how old and anxious her eyes were. How she needed a counselor, not a man, and how I had failed her, and myself.

I want to believe I'm different now. I want to believe that my judgment is better, that Aya will not suffer from my shortcomings or misguided instincts …

… It all started a few months ago, when my wife and I went to Aya Dane's gallery exhibit—which would turn out to be her last. When I saw her artwork, I was touched in ways I'd never been before. In it I saw proof of a shadowy dance between talent, exile and mental illness. I saw a return of the repressed, in an age of barren windows and flat screens. And in the corner of her every canvas, her signature—a blood-red flower, waiting to bloom—there was hope, too.

After the exhibit, as Catherine and I were leaving the gallery, we heard sounds of a scuffle coming from the alleyway behind the building. We could see a woman, trapped, being attacked by two men, their faces covered by white masks.

We ran partway down the alley to confront them, yelling that the police were on their way. The men were startled and stopped. As we came closer, the men scaled the chain-link fence at the end of the alley and ran off. Before they slipped away, I saw that their arms and hands were bleeding, that the young woman had fought back against her assailants.

As Catherine helped the woman up, we could see she'd been hurt. I looked at her face. It seemed familiar to me. I tried to get a better look at her as I smoothed her tangled hair from her eyes. Suddenly, I recognized her. So did Catherine. She was the artist whose showing we had just been to.

We took her to the hospital and stayed with her there until the doctors told us that her injuries were not serious. They said it was a good thing we'd passed by the alley when we did, for if we hadn't, it could have been much worse.

Before we left, I gave her my card and told her I was a psychiatrist, that I could help her. That she should come see me.

That was how I first met Aya Dane …

… She came to see me shortly after that. I didn't recognize her at first. She'd cropped her hair, she was wafer thin…The first visit, she didn't finish the hour. She ran out in the middle of our session. It was weeks before she came back.

When she did return, she was shaking like a leaf. She told me she couldn't paint anymore. That she'd lost her most treasured painting, that she needed to rest, gather strength, heal. Each time I asked her a question, she answered in the third person. When I asked her, "Who is speaking for Aya Dane?" her voice answered, "I am she. I speak for and protect Aya Dane when she is resting. I shelter her."

I asked her to agree to spend some time here at the Center, for her own good. I believed she couldn't safely function in the world and needed around-the-clock medical and psychiatric care. I assured her that she'd never be treated as a prisoner, that her talent and privacy would be protected, that the Cambridge Center was a progressive facility. She'd enjoy a certain level of freedom, to express herself in different ways, to come and go as needed, as earned, as mutually defined. It would be for a period of time only, and once she overcame her current crisis, she could function once more in the outside world.

Even as I gave my professional recommendation, as a doctor, I couldn't help but feel something for her, as a man, and these feelings scared me.

Aya revealed that she had been in chronic pain for many years, suffering from acute and often disorienting states. In the past months, she began to lapse into psychotic episodes of greater or lesser severity. She began to show symptoms of paranoia and diffuse memory loss. Although she had hallucinations and delusions. I ruled out schizophrenia and concluded that her illness was primarily a dissociative disorder, a product of trauma, and isolation.

To treat her, I used a mix of therapeutic tools, some cutting edge, and others, more traditional. I prescribed an array of neuroleptic and antianxiety medications. I also applied deep transcranial magnetic stimulation to the parts of the brain that have been shown to be responsible for delusions and hallucinations. The patient often fainted after these treatments, which may have been a side effect of the TMS.

I continued to have daily sessions with Aya. As weeks went on, the voice speaking for her became more present and dominant. Her stories were still filled with patchworks of real

*and imagined encounters, still told with the dissociated "she,"
and I started to doubt the therapy's efficacy. Where was Aya
Dane? Where was she hiding?*

*There was some measure of success in the fact that she'd
started painting again. Not much, and only portraits. Still, it
was a small step in reopening her to the world.*

*But any measure of success was difficult to quantify. One
of my failures was my inability to identify the source of her
creativity. Her art was the thick rope knotting together her
identity and her pathology. It was, at the same time, her illness and her cure. Her "absolution," as she once told me.*

*If I could get her to reconnect the threads of her being
and her creativity, I could perhaps help her rebuild her self,
as much as what is broken can ever be mended. But it was a
dangerous undertaking. Where did her illness end and her art
begin? Wherein lay the cure?*

*It was then that I asked her to write down her story, from
as far back as she could remember to the present. To write
what she pleased, as long as the subject was herself, Aya Dane.
I hoped that writing, like her artwork, would allow her to
emerge, to actively engage with the world as her real self. But,
when I finally got her notebook in my hands, it was written
in the third person.*

*Despite what I perceived as the failure of my experiment,
through her writing I was able to identify another symptom.
To the catchall diagnosis of dissociative disorder, I could add
my own long-sought personal discovery: exile syndrome.*

*Aya Dane is obsessed with the past, and memory—or its
loss. She is filled with and guided by an acute, unbearable
nostalgia, accompanied by the presence of intrusive, overpowering images—in Aya's case, the harrowing image of the sea
as a mass grave.*

I began to search for what may have triggered the dissociation and the delusions that accompanied it. In the brain scans, I found that the patient's brain, visibly affected by her past trauma, had succumbed to an unbearable trigger when she was a young girl. Her symptoms were likely exacerbated by her experiences as an immigrant, an Arab, a Muslim woman in a world often hostile to people like her. I believe that, given different circumstances, her psychosis could have been kept in check.

I recognized some of these same symptoms in my own grandmother, Beck Vandeer—or Rebecca Yacov. It was only after her death that I even learned her real name. At the end of her life, Beck was eaten up by returning memories of the old country. They hollowed her out until she lost her mind. One day, while walking the grounds of the Center together, I told Aya about her and about her beautiful summer home in Martha's Vineyard. I also told her that my grandmother reminded me of her, in some of her expressions, her postures.

I also knew that Aya had been close to an old Ashkenazi Jewish woman, also a Rebecca—Rebecca Innlaender—who had been admitted here, on and off for over thirty years. I knew how sad Aya had been when hearing of her passing. The portrait she did of her now hung in the front entrance of the hospital. It was not a far stretch for her to create a mix of these two Rebeccas. What was most strange was that I could see hints of my grandmother in Aya Dane's portrait of Rebecca Innlaender. My grandmother, a woman Aya had never seen, yet had managed to capture.

From Aya's notebook, I could see how she could have collaged those conversations and transformed them into a joyous fairy tale of a moment. I felt both pride and sadness that an individual like Aya Dane could construct a fantasy from my family. From myself.

… She read one passage about me choosing her over Catherine. Perhaps I shouldn't have told her about my wife and our recent coldness toward one another. I may even have used the words "estranged" and "loveless" to describe our relationship, which may have been confusing to her, as well as crossing professional boundaries.

Other conversations Aya mentioned in her journal were a patchwork gleaned from here and there, some from her life in Boston and some from her placement in the Center. Some seemed loosely based on exchanges we'd had during our sessions and had a semblance of truth, which she then curbed to fit her delusions.

As for Ari, he might or might not have been real. The art world has its own mysterious characters and arcane secrets that I'm not privy to. After all, my world, too, abounds with secret clubs and mysterious societies. Does Aya believe him to be real? I'm not sure …

… After speaking to Michel Abensour Stirling, I became convinced that Aya's memories of the old country were probably more rooted in truth than her depicted present.

I found the number of Abensour Stirling, who still resided in Tangiers and was close to meeting his maker, through friends of friends who had known his father, the famous American poet James Stirling. I called the number in Tangiers and was surprised to be answered by a cultured voice with a strange English accent, a mix between an old-fashioned New England accent and an unplaceable foreign one, perhaps Spanish. There were cackles and breaks in his speech, high-pitched intonations that punctuated his sentences in odd places.

Michel Abensour Stirling confirmed that he had known Aya Dane. That he had taken her in to atone for the great

wrong he had once done her, perhaps even to atone for the great
wrong his own father had done him in abandoning him and
his mother.

He also confirmed that Aya's parents had perished in a
fire. But the arsonist had never been confirmed. There were
rumors that Aya's brother Kareem had been responsible for the
fire.

And he admitted that he had sent text messages to Aya.
No, nothing cryptic. Simple messages asking how she was do-
ing, once a year, on the anniversary of the day she came to live
with him. But she never replied. He was glad to know she had
received them.

But Kareem, he said, had disappeared. He may well have
come to see her, like Aya claimed, for he may have survived
crossing the sea clandestinely to emigrate to Europe, or he may
have returned from fighting in Syria or Iraq. No one really
knew where he'd been …

… I felt a peculiar pang of jealousy toward this Abensour
Stirling, who had known Aya when she was so young and
vulnerable. So absolutely desirable, I imagined …

… Aya could leave the Center if she chose to, and I wondered
how long she would remain. As I spent more time with her, I
began to have a terrifying thought—how long would I be able
to see her, talk to her, hold her in? …

… This case has placed in front of me my own doubts, my own
self. I believe—despite my medical training—that those who
emigrate to the States, and are lucky enough to succeed, should
feel blessed, proud, to have made it here, as part of the most
highly achieving nation in the world. And this belief, which I

didn't know to be so entrenched in me, before treating Aya, has further strained my sense of professional responsibility toward her.

After months with little apparent progress, I see no choice but to conclude that the therapy has been a failure. I can see that I went too far, but I can't confide in anyone. The consequences would be too great. This experience, this experiment, has exhausted me. To survive, to distract myself from the love I may have felt for her but could never let anyone know, I remind myself of the life I've built, my place in the world, my accomplishments. I think of people's stares when I walk down the street with Catherine at my arm.

And yet, she haunts me. Being with her reminded me of my boyhood, of a childhood I never had, of a love never given by those closest to me. Sometimes, at night, in the warmth of my marital bed, in the secrecy of night, my wife asleep next to me, our little son in the room next door, I think of Aya Dane, of what life might have been like with a woman like her.

But she was an immigrant, an Arab, and…well, they aren't like us. They have their own mental illnesses—odd, crooked, monstrous variations of female hysteria. I know hysteria is an unmentionable, unacceptable diagnosis now. But whatever name they gave it, its existence can't be denied.

During our sessions, I sometimes felt ill at the scent of decay that always seemed to accompany her. I felt physically disgusted by her, repelled, as though I'd just had a whiff of carrion scent that was so far removed from my wife's healthy, citrusy scent.

Tonight, I will lean toward Catherine, asleep at my side. Her breathing will be serene and quiet. I will lay my head on the pillow, and think mundane thoughts. Catherine will open her eyes, and we will both pretend that nothing has happened, that everything is as it always has been, that there are no cracks in our marriage.

I will put Aya Dane's decay, her loss and sadness, behind me. She was a strange, exotic fantasy, nothing more ...

———

The recording became unclear, robotic, undecipherable static. Then, the tape finally stopped and the recorder ejected it.

There was something old-fashioned and decrepit in the manner that Dr. Vandeer depicted my mental state. A nostalgia of his own, perhaps. I was his Dora, his poem, his experiment, his breakthrough, his work of art, his fraud.

I removed the magnetic tape from the recorder, and breathed.

The cold barrenness surrounding me had receded into something else, something elusive and precious, which appeared from the broken pieces.

A soft quiet, and a rush of color.

thirty-nine

For the first time in many blood-red moons, I thought about what it meant to be free, and I yearned for a life beyond the odd, crooked house that had been my home, my prison, for the past months in this country. I reached into my pocket, found my phone, dialed a number. I whispered into the phone—a number, an address, a car.

I couldn't fully understand my brokenness, nor where it would take me, but it had taken me this far. I closed my eyes and listened to my Malian friend play the Saheli blues on his guitar. I listened to the notes of deft beauty and skill that he coaxed from the strings. He seemed to be saying to me, "Leave, leave, Aya Dane, *ma soeur, ma douce*, my sister, my sweet. Leave while you still can, while the noose is not yet wound tightly around your neck."

His words reminded me that I wasn't anyone's prisoner. I wrapped my fast brightening scarf, now abloom with wild flowers, around me and left. In the dead of night, when everything was quiet and swaying gently in the moonlight, when all were asleep, or pretending to be.

No one knew I was going except for Dr. David Vandeer. At first he tried to tell me I wasn't yet ready to leave, that I still needed him. But when confronted with his dented tape recorder—his confession—he stepped aside, even opened a door, a wrought-iron gate for me, in a silent plea for forgiveness.

As I left, I turned to look back at the silent house one last time and thought I saw him standing at the window, surrounded in shadow, looking down at me. I wondered at the thoughts that must haunt him, must keep him awake, in his home, in his work, in the dead of night.

I wondered what Catherine might be thinking, beyond the great divide. Is she having trouble sleeping at night, too? Does she lie awake and wonder if the world is large enough to lose me, or small enough to ever find me?

I turn away and look ahead. The air I breathe is fresh and clean, the air of an unmarked path. I breathe it in a second time. It has a distinct scent, of moist earth and young buds, of greenness, of youth, of light, of things unknown to me. Its strangeness is exhilarating.

forty

You close my words now. You know everything about me. I may never know who you are, but I have some suspicions about who you must be, how you think of me, who you are hiding behind.

If it's you, holding these words between your hands, who has already betrayed me once, who has sat in my chair, then understand I'm giving this to you as my deliverance, not as my surrender. You'll read what I think of you. You will see how, in the end, after you thought I was broken beyond measure, I liberated myself from you, became myself once more—fragmented, torn, but undeniably one.

I push aside these swirling thoughts and instead I dream, I hope beyond hope, that you, who are reading these lines, are my mother. You have just made your syrupy sweet mint tea and you are sitting in my chair that is your chair, first, Mother. You cradle my notebook in your hands, as though it were I, when I was a child, and afraid of the dark. You soothe me and calm my fear of the night and the unknown. You put your hands on my face. You stroke my hair and tell me, over and over, that you will come with me into the deepest, darkest darkness. That you will be there with me at the bottom of the sea, waiting for it all to pass.

And you will never know you are already forgiven. I have forgiven you a long time ago. For your strength, for being the woman on a forbidden beach who strayed too far. For your weakness. For a father thinned and weakened by time, by the love you took away from him. For Kareem. For giving me up to Abensour Stirling. For the fire. For me.

Who can tell what strange fruit exile will plant in the hearts and minds of its unwilling wanderers? As Abensour Stirling once told me, speaking of his mother's people, the great Abensours of Tangiers, and of their centennial wanderings through Europe, North Africa, the Middle and the Far Easts and now the Americas, "There is no joyful exile, only fruit after bitter fruit before the long-awaited relief of death." He says this to me as he drinks his wine and eats his oranges, sitting in his wicker chair, in his white-and-blue tiled terrace.

Perhaps Abensour Stirling imagined that the best thing to befall someone like me was to share his fate. That the best I could hope for would be to one day sit in his wicker chair, drink his wine, eat his oranges and stretch my tired feet on his tiled terrace.

Maybe that was what Ari wanted from me, as well. To spread his desires and hunger over mine and draw the line between the old and the new, to murder me and extinguish my voice. But that will not be so.

I have given up the *Aya Dane*, the darkened tea grains, the whites, blues and browns of Tangiers, the muñeca, the lullabies my mother sang to me as a child, the promises made but not kept, the unwanted embraces, the image of bodies washing up on the shore. The fear, the anger and guilt.

I have surrendered my painting, but not myself. The memories that spoke to me, and for me, no longer hold me in their sway. They are swirls, whirlpools, flashes, dimness and darkness at the back of my mind, at the edge of me, but no longer out of reach. They are poised to become color and lines, paint and matter, once more.